MW01609112

CRAVING MY BOSS

TASHA FAWKES

M. S. PARKER

SAFIRA PUBLISHING, LLC

Copyright © 2017 Tasha Fawkes & M. S. Parker

Published by Safira Publishing LLC

ISBN-13: 978-1-941837-46-7

ISBN-10: 1-941837-46-8

CONTENTS

down on her back into the tangle of velvet sheets. Her lover followed her down, his blond hair damp with perspiration, his jaw clenched from the immense effort it took to hold himself back, his fierce green eyes promising swift correction for her mistake. She trembled beneath him as his animalistic gaze raked her. To him, she was a tantalizing dish of trussed-up limbs, a womanly feast who had no choice but to spread for him and let him end her torment with a thrust of his majestic...

"Ashley!"

I rocket out of my chair in the break room, the effect of hearing my name like a splash of cold water dumped on the proceedings. I slam the screen of my laptop down quickly as Tory Keppel, inconvenient coworker, strides into the kitchen.

"I believe the word you are looking for is 'manhood'? Or something similar? Or maybe something more contemporary," she offers as she pulls up the chair beside me and drops down.

I flush, my tongue as tied as my heroine, but I can't think of a good deflection to throw her off the scent. If she managed to read even a line of my book—

"You're describing Daniel, right?"

"No!" My protest sounds strangled and comes too readily to be believed. Tory raises a strawberry-blonde eyebrow at me. "I mean... am I?" I feign surprise as I pick at a loose thread on the hem of my skirt. *"I hadn't noticed."*

"I mean, I know they tell us to 'write what we know'

in every pithy college creative writing class, but *wow*." Tory whistles. "There's no way you can know *that* much about our boss."

"I..." My throat has gone completely dry. Unlike the roll I was on a minute ago, the right words simply won't come. "... Please don't tell anyone, Tory. Especially Stewart," I plead. "It's just something I'm writing for fun."

I hope the amused twist to Tory's smile bodes well for me, even if her eyes are skeptical. Stewart, my on-again off-again hookup of two years, is also Tory's cousin. Stewart *definitely* doesn't know about my private prose sessions.

"All right. I won't tell," Tory promises.

My posture relaxes instantly, and it's all I can do to keep from slipping down in my chair and puddling onto the break room floor. "Thank you." I breathe a sigh of relief.

"But that tied-up girl is totally you, isn't she?"

I manage a sheepish grin as I collect my laptop and rise. It's all for Tory's benefit—because her conclusion is terrifying in its truth, and I don't want her to know just how personal that last passage is. Better to put on a show of having come to terms with being caught than give over to the stark panic raging inside of me. I'm confident that for the sake of my relationship with Stewart, she'll keep things between us.

What relationship? The little voice in the back of my mind niggles dismally as I stride down the hall toward the small office I share with Tory and another editor.

My desk stands in front of the window. Things with Stewart had been—have been—tepid from the start, and that start was two years ago. 'Tepid' is *definitely* an adjective I wouldn't use in my novel—so why have I made any space for it in my life?

I played up my relationship with Stewart to Tory twice to save my own skin. The truth is, I don't consider what we have as a 'relationship'—but he does.

What I consider a relationship, I'm finding is a lot more intense than most people can comfortably stomach.

I sit down behind my desk. Pen and Quill Publishing is a casual, open-door kind of publishing house. I don't know why I thought that coveted concept of privacy could be found in the break room today. I pop open my laptop, my eyes skimming over what I've written, before hitting Save and exiling my manuscript back to the hidden folder I keep on my desktop.

Tory is right. My novel's nameless hero is none other than Daniel Stone, the company CEO. Our boss. *My* boss. The descriptors I've employed in every hot passage so far point directly to my muse. It'd probably be a good idea to update some detail—*any* detail—to make it less obvious, but somehow, I can't bring myself to render the changes. I *want* the hero to be Daniel Stone. And I want that bound, shuddering, gasping little sub begging for release beneath him to be me.

Somehow, I thought putting words to my most inti-mate fantasies would get them out of my system. No way that sort of relationship is possible—not with Stewart, and definitely not with Daniel, the multi-millionaire who barely remembers my name, but it's only gotten worse since I started writing, and now I find I can't stop. I'm hopelessly addicted to the plight of my raven-haired heroine, and I'm way too invested in the forms her punishments take.

Maybe it's the close call with Tory that makes me more sympathetic than usual to queries from prospective authors today. I tab open my inbox and start replying to e-mails, avoiding my usual stock pleasantries and copy-pasted form rejections and focusing a little more on encouragement than usual. *You might try querying at The Lifted Kilt Literary Agency,* I advise one aspiring historical romance writer. *Here is the contact info for one of their newer agents who is in the market for writers like you to represent! Feel free to use me as a reference. While our own preferences at this time lean more toward the contemporary, you'll have an easier go of querying in the future once you've locked in an agent. Best of luck!*

"Knock, knock."

I glanced up from my latest dispatch. Elektra Ahladiotis, the firm's senior editor, leans in the doorway. Elektra is a petite older woman in her fifties, although she doesn't look it with that jet-black hair of hers and beautiful skin. She speaks with just a hint of her native Greece, which lends her voice a scintillating quality as exotic as her looks. She's Daniel's right-hand woman, and a formidable force of nature that I feel lucky to work directly beside most days.

"How is my assistant today?"

I'm not only Elektra's assistant, but the editorial assistant to every other editor at Pen and Quill; still, what resources Elektra decides to command, Elektra gets. That includes me.

"Good." I hit the Send tab on my latest e-mail and lean back in my chair, trying to school my expression to something carefully neutral even though my heart thuds erratically in my chest. Any unexpected appearance by Elektra usually makes my mind *and* pulse race with worry about having missed some minor editing detail, but today is worse than usual. Has Tory mentioned my pet project to her? Maybe I should've reiterated that she was to tell *nobody*. Maybe I should've made her sign a contract in blood. Maybe I should just start looking for another job since my career at Pen and Quill is as good as over.

"I just wanted to check in with you about the Christmas party this coming Saturday," Elektra says. "As I recall, you were put in charge of food. I haven't heard anything about it recently, so I assume it's taken care of."

She peers over her spectacles at me with those flinty dark eyes of hers, and it's all I can do to not breathe an audible sigh of relief. All thoughts of living in my car with only my manuscript to keep me warm evaporate. "I've got it locked in," I confirm. "Daniel's... Mister Stone's favorite restaurant has agreed to cater."

"Maurelli's?"

I nod. Elektra's sharp gaze warms approvingly. "Your attention to detail has once more been noted, Ashley. Not many of Mister Stone's employees make it their business to know his preferences. He is sure to be pleased."

I nod again, more to hide the heat flooding my cheeks than anything. Of course, I made it my business to know Daniel's preferences. Calling Maurelli's was one of the first things I did when I learned *he* would be attending the party, and it hadn't been an easy gig to secure. There's a cunning quality to Elektra's look now that makes me think this latest evidence of my devotion is sure to trickle back to him.

"You've done well, Ashley. I'll leave you to it." Elektra raps her knuckle on my desk in parting and glides back down the hall. Once I'm sure she's gone, I do a gleeful spin in my chair. I have no delusions about Daniel's availability, especially to someone like *me,* but I can't deny how goddamn good it feels to succeed on even this minor front. And who knows? I might even get an acknowledgement Saturday from the big man himself.

Big man...

The thought triggers a mental image I could definitely use in my novel. "You need help, Ashley," I mutter through a dreamy smile. I focus on work then, making sure I've caught up with all my e-mails before I click open the hidden folder. At the very least, I have time to finish that last paragraph before—

My work cell chimes. Text message. I'm still looking at the Word document, at all that empty space that needs filling—at that mewling heroine who needs filling most of all—when I thumb it open. I grimace when I see who the texts are from.

Stewart: Yo!

Stewart: Want me to come over tonight and help you relieve some stress?

Stewart: You've earned it. ;)

Stewart: I had us penciled in for some sexy times so just let me know. Also wanted to confirm the time of the holiday party this Saturday.

Stewart: Can't wait to see you!

My inspiration shrivels. I close my laptop and mull over how to respond, which ends with me just staring blankly out an office window. How to reply? *I told you not to text me at this number? We're not in a relationship. I've told you a thousand times to quit acting like we are.*

I used to think it wasn't Stewart's fault he couldn't take a hint, but now I'm not so sure. I've been pretty clear on this front, and his unwillingness to recognize my waning interest—or to even *listen* to me when I tell him outright that I need more in the bedroom and less during the light of day—is starting to wear on me. I don't like being the salacious, it's-only-sex-between-us villain in Stewart's life story, but maybe that's who I am at the end of the day.

Good girls certainly don't daydream about whips and chains and a healthy dose of mind-blowing pleasure with their pain.

Am I the villain? I stare at Stewart's unanswered texts. The more I find myself able to put words and meaning to what I want, the more liberated I feel and less certain who I might hurt in the process.

There's one thing I know, at least. I'm not afraid if the one who winds up bruised and begging is me.

2

DANIEL

"Daniel!"

The woman beneath me screams. It's the way I prefer to hear my own name: in the form of a helpless plea; an explosive cry; a shapeless, senseless appeal for me to pull the trigger and end her suffering. But suffering is what Crystal loves. It's why she comes to me.

And why she comes *for* me.

"Not yet," I growl, leaning over the sweat-soaked, shuddering plane of my sub's back. I thrust my thick cock between the cheeks of her perfect ass, burying myself to the hilt again and again as I take her from behind. Her magnificent breasts bounce with the force of the rhythm I dictate, catching and scattering the papers on my desk.

Crystal is the reason my office at Pen and Quill is soundproof. We've been going at it for almost an hour now, and her wails increase in volume as I come up with new and creative ways to make her beg for it. Getting fucked this hard from behind takes her to the absolute limit of her endurance, and I'm not about to let her off easy after one or two plaintive calls for mercy.

Crystal's visit caught me unaware today—a surprise worthy of the punishment she's receiving—but I don't have the usual tools at my disposal. But I'm not her Dom due to my lack of imagination. I pull harder on the belt I've used to cinch her wrists behind her back, and she arches with a sweet little moan of compliance. I only need one hand to fist the belt around; I bury the other in her rich brown curls and yank her head back so I can get a better look at her expression. Her pretty face is contorted in ecstasy, her eyebrows pulled together until they can't possibly climb any higher. I break my rhythm to thrust into her unexpectedly and watch her wince. She wasn't ready that time. Her mouth drops open again and she tries her best to look over her shoulder, which requires her to fight against her restraints. Those big brown eyes almost dare to look outraged.

I live for the little rises, the fleeting challenges to my authority, that I get out of Crystal. They don't come often enough for my taste.

And my tastes are voracious.

"Too hard for you?" I taunt. I punch my hips into her and watch as her tits press against the polished wood surface beneath her. "You're the best thing to pass across my desk all day."

"Fuck me, Master!" she pants. Hearing that word on her cherry-red lips both thrills and annoys me, as it should. Crystal's not the one who gets to make demands in this relationship, and she knows it.

"You should see yourself right now." I crane closer, winding her thick locks tight enough around my fingers to straighten that girlish curl right out of them. "You flounced in here this afternoon like you owned the place, but we both know I'm the one who owns *you*. If you could see the way my cock now fills your tight little pussy... maybe *then* you'd remember who's calling the shots."

"I'm going to *come*," Crystal moans, dragging the word out in a hum. My cell rings, and I debate whether or not to let her achieve a final release before picking up. Letting it go to voicemail isn't an option, especially not when I see my fiancée's name on the caller ID.

Crystal's discarded panties are conveniently within reach. I grab them, ball them up tight, and stick them between those protesting, voluptuous lips of hers. She clamps down obediently, wide eyes imploring, but I need her quiet. I wrench the belt that binds her wrists, testing my improvised gag as I use my other hand to pluck my phone off the desk. Her answering squeal is muffled to my satisfaction. I slide my cock all the way in to reward her as I answer the call.

"Daniel here."

"How's work?" Karen Queen, mother-approved fiancée, asks, her voice sounding bored.

I eye Crystal's pretty, splayed form beneath me and

grin. She wiggles in alarm at that grin. "Oh, you know. Same as always. Chained to my desk today."

Or at least someone is.

"I just wanted to make sure you hadn't forgotten our dinner plans tonight."

Her voice is disapproving, as usual, like she's already made up her mind that I have. Which, balls-deep in Crystal, I definitely have.

"Dinner." I don't give her the satisfaction of hearing the question in my voice as I glance over to scan for my day planner. One of Crystal's earlier thrashes must have sent it toppling to the floor. "Of course, I haven't forgotten."

"Good," she says. "Because I don't intend to be left alone with your mother yet *again*. With all the wedding planning your absences are forcing *us* to get done, I might as well be marrying *her*."

Beneath me, Crystal makes a muffled noise—apparently, she can hear every word that Karen says on the other end. I give her restraints a warning tug, and she arches her back in cat-like pleasure as my cock brushes up against her secret inner spot.

"I haven't forgotten, and I don't intend to," I tell Karen. "I'll be there."

God knows I don't want to be. Maybe fucking Crystal is what's gotten me into a domineering mood at present, but I want to tell Karen—and my mother—that I'll be available to plan a wedding precisely when I have the time and desire to do so. Which may be never.

Instead, I find myself agreeing to meet them wherever it is we planned to meet. I mentally detach from the bland conversation with Karen and my thoughts drift, going beyond even the four walls of my office and the reality of the naked woman beneath me. Listening to myself talk to Karen is like listening to a man going through the motions of a life that he knows isn't worth living. It's a depressing thought, but one I've resigned myself to.

I don't love Karen. Karen doesn't love me. I don't love Crystal. Crystal doesn't love me. We all have requirements that need to be satisfied. Karen knows I see other women, and it doesn't bother her so long as I keep things purely physical. Crystal knows I'm not interested in anything other than sex. It's a perfect system. It should satisfy my need for control. Then why does it all feel so pointless?

"All right. We'll be expecting you at seven."

Karen signs off without a real parting word, but it doesn't matter. I'm sure that later, we'll pick up wherever we left off. I toss my phone down onto my desk and rein Crystal in. I remove the panties from between her teeth, and she sucks in a lungful of air.

"Everything all right?"

I glance down into those big brown eyes and debate whether or not to answer her. Then again, there's nothing substantive I can tell her when I don't know the answer myself.

I stick to our script. I release my grip on the belt and let her fight the restraints as much as she wants as I pound her into the desk. Soon she's crying out once more, senseless with need, a slave to the whims of her body and a tool for my sexual release.

And for a fleeting moment, it almost does feel right.

~

"... well, I'm glad that you're at least picking up *Karen's* calls now while you're at work," my mother comments while she swirls cabernet in her wine glass.

I watch the ruby-red whirlpool that forms, trapped within the bowl. I wait for even a single drop to escape; to slosh out over the edge and form a hundred-dollar stain on the restaurant's impeccable white tablecloth. It never does.

Shannon Stone is good at avoiding potentially messy situations.

My mother is young at sixty-eight, made younger by countless plastic surgeries and rejuvenating treatments that she diverts all my father's leftover fortune toward. I don't see the point of the practice, personally. No one is immune to the ravages of time, and my mother's poised, petrified face is no exception.

Karen can talk with my mother for hours long stretches about the latest beauty breakthroughs and cleansing tricks. I almost wish they would find the time to talk about it now. Instead, my mother appears insistent on bringing up Pen and Quill. She never approved of my embarking on my publishing venture, and she still doesn't approve, even after I agreed to remain CEO of Stone Exports. The look of measured disdain around the edges of her mouth isn't something even her most highly-paid plastic surgeons can get rid of.

"I'm in and out of a lot of meetings, Mother," I reply. It isn't a lie. Crystal's sweating, sublime body comes to mind as I recall our latest meeting.

"He's delegating more," Karen offers.

She leans over in her chair to wrap a hand around my forearm. I tolerate it, but just barely. She knows what she's going to marry: a classically handsome, physically fit, statuesque poster boy who can't seem to shake the stuffy smell of old New York money or the bloodhounds that pursue it. She's going to marry into a multi-million-dollar fortune generations in the making, just the way her daddy always wanted.

And what do I get out of our arrangement of convenience? Political connections. Like I give a damn. Mother couldn't be happier, of course. She may rail against my involvement with Pen and Quill, but what she really wants is for me to run for office. Even Stone Exports comes secondary to her true ambitions.

But what do *I* get out of it? I'm Daniel Stone the Third, the third in my family to own the name and the shrewd business savvy that comes with it. It doesn't even take a Stone to see that I'm getting the short end of the stick. I don't want to go into politics. I can barely manage to work up the interest to deal with Stone Exports. Maybe, if I'm lucky, I'll finally get some peace and quiet—and some much-needed privacy to pursue the off-hours recreation that actually satisfies me.

I watch Karen charm my mother. She regales her with an amusing anecdote about how she was forced to fire the latest wedding planner last weekend when she noticed the other woman looking at me in a way she didn't like. My mother laughs and comes back with a similar story of her own. Karen leans harder into me, and I'm certain we must appear exactly as she hopes: close, cohesive, and head-over-heels in love.

I could muster a smile, but I don't bother. The two women won't expect it—they won't even look for it. I'm a man in control of everything and nothing.

Concessions. Compromise. That's all life is for me now; the pursuit of meaningless victories and the manufactured enjoyment of their empty rewards. I've been splitting my attention and bending over backward to accommodate everyone for so long that I'm not certain that *isn't* how things are supposed to shake out in the end.

That doesn't keep me from wishing I could get out of this goddamn marriage.

3

ASHLEY

"No, I... yes, that will be fine."

I pinch my nose, needing a light reminder that this is the incompetent reality I inhabit. The woman on the other line—who purports to be Maurelli's manager—tells me that she'll make up for the missing vegetarian lasagna with a full refund on half the order, and have an additional dessert sent over from the restaurant.

The mishap doesn't matter too much in the long run. All around me, the Pen and Quill Christmas party is in full swing: authors, agents, and editors mill about the lavish center table, too busy throwing back wine and talking animatedly with one another to fill their mouths with much else. There's less than two hundred bodies in attendance, and I haven't heard anything from a single disgruntled vegetarian yet, so I'm almost ready to call the evening a success.

Then Stewart arrives.

"Babe! Babe!"

Stewart waves at me from the doorway and manages to slosh the champagne he's ferrying over onto the floor. He smiles sheepishly at me when he arrives and tries to pass the empty flute to me anyway.

"Don't you think you've had enough?" I hiss, looking around to see if anyone is watching. I'm so embarrassed. I snatch the other full flute from him and chug it down before Elektra looks my way. Thankfully, she appears preoccupied with a client and has completely missed my humiliation. Stewart offers a grin, oblivious to my mortification.

"Nope. I still feel out of place amid all your fancy publishing friends."

That's because you are out of place! I want to scream. *I didn't invite you! I didn't want a plus one!*

What I *wanted* was a moment alone with Daniel Stone, who still hasn't shown his dead-sexy self as far as I know. What I *wanted* was to *not* be called *babe* in front of all my fancy publishing friends. Stewart's smile straightens itself out a little when he finally notes what I hope is a dour look of disapproval, but there's no coming back from how much he's managed to put down in the first half hour of the party, and from what I suspect he imbibed the hour before.

Stewart Beecham is not my boyfriend. He is not *my* babe. He's not even this annoying normally—at least, not in this overbearing, socially awkward way that I'm now forced to deal with. Stewart is a pathologist. He's normally so clinical, so boring and specific... about *everything.* It's structure without control; it's lists upon lists of itemized ways to be intimate with one another, yet at the end of the day they're all as bland as soft serve vanilla ice cream. No sprinkles, no Gummies, no chocolate or strawberry syrup. Just... boring.

"Well, why don't you go try to talk to someone who isn't me?" I grab Stewart by the shoulders and steer him toward the nearest conversation, broadcasting a psychic apology to the two women as I do so. "I need a break. I need... I need to find the bathroom."

He nods as I thread my way through the revelers, sighing with relief. I need some fresh air. I need—

"I love you!" Stewart hollers.

Oh God. I stiffen with another bout of mortification as I dart from the room. Just outside the doorway in the hall, I realize that the heels I wore aren't made for darting, and my left ankle buckles. I barely manage to catch my balance as I keep moving. I manage to make it out of the hallway and into my small office. I slam the door closed and lean against it, eyes closed, shaking my head.

I breathe a heavy sigh of relief into the cool, familiar darkness of my safe harbor. I took on way too much tonight, and what for? So I could try to impress a man who couldn't even be bothered to show to his own company party? I try to muster some anger at Daniel Stone as I move to my desk and collapse down into the chair, but all I really feel is aching disappointment.

I let my mind drift to him now. I imagine him

finding me here, alone in my office, sheathed in the bright red dress I had rented out for the evening—the one that sober Stewart had called outlandish. But I knew what I wanted. Red is the color that signals passion louder than all the rest. Daniel would know this. He wouldn't be able to tear his eyes from me—or keep them from falling, lower, lower, even as he asked me what was wrong...

I open my laptop and have the Word document pulled up before I realize what I'm doing. The glow from the screen is comforting, my characters familiar, keeping me company. The hero would never skip a party when he knew the heroine would be in attendance. He would never be able to overlook her to begin with.

I'm halfway through a revision of an earlier scene —really an expansion into a passionate sex scene, the hero and heroine seizing a much-needed break in the plot's drama to relieve the tension that's built between them—when the door to my office eases open.

I know better than to freak out now like I did the last time. My fingers pause above the keyboard, and I raise my eyes to the intruder. Stewart enters and grabs the chair from Tory's desk and pulls it closer to mine. He smells sweetly-sour, like the champagne he's been drinking all evening. His eyes shimmer, but his expression is sober.

Uh-oh.

"What's up, Stewart?" I push my laptop to the side,

but leave it open to let him know he's interrupting something I intend to finish. He gazes at me from beneath his shaggy brown hair, and I'm not sure he's noticed my signal. It wouldn't be the first time.

"I want to talk about us," he says, point blank. "I think it's time to put a name to what we are. I love you, Ash."

"I... know that you've said that before." I wince at my own indelicate response. "But I'm happy with what we are. I don't see why we have to give it a name."

"You're avoiding having this conversation." Stewart frowns.

My eyes narrow.

"Maybe because the depth of your feelings for me makes you uncomfortable? I know you've had relationships in the past, Ash, but how meaningful were they, really?"

I gaze at him in disbelief. "Yes. I've had relationships." And maybe I thought they meant something at the time, but now I can see how hopelessly lacking they all were. That's the whole reason I resisted becoming anything more with Stewart from the beginning. I thought I was finally waking up to what I wanted, but now I feel that Stewart is trying to lull me back to sleep. Complacency. I shake my head.

"I just want you to know it's okay to feel like you want to settle down with me, Ash," Stewart continues.

He leans across the desk and takes my hand in his. I let him. Usually I'm encouraged by any lead he decides to take, no matter how small. But not this time. I wait.

"So, let's settle down together. I'm drunk, but you know what I mean. Let's settle. Be boyfriend and girlfriend."

Settle. Settle. Settle. The lone word echoes in my head, knocking against empty passages that should hold all the worthwhile memories I have of my time with Stewart. Why can't I recall a single instance of feeling satisfied?

"You mean you want to make it official?" I finally ask, my voice barely above a whisper.

Stewart grins. He's handsome when he does that. Hell, he's handsome most of the time.

"Yeah. Settled," he agrees, or at least thinks he's agreeing.

I yank my hand from his. "Stewart, how much more 'settled' can we get?" I ask, my voice ringing with frustration. I rise from my chair, and a belated moment later, he mirrors me. I square off with him from across my desk, bracing myself for the outpouring of words I've been meaning to say for so long. I gush it all out. "You make *lists* that have to do with foreplay! Don't think I haven't seen them. *Spend no more than five minutes performing oral sex before confirming readiness for penetration.* Really?"

"I read that in a journal!" he quickly defends. "Published in a prestigious paper! I thought it was sound advice. *You* seemed to like it at the time."

How can I tell him I'd faked it? I resist the urge to

tug my hair out in annoyance. I settle for grinding my teeth and pinching my nose for the umpteenth time this evening. "It's the same thing over and over with you," I continue, not unkindly. "I don't want lists, Stewart, even of the things I like—and, by the way, that is way too brief a session of oral for any sexually mature individual to get *anything* worthwhile out of it. I want more than just clinical biology. I don't want to be examined, or tested, or... or..." I wave a hand, mentally erasing what I just said. It doesn't matter. He won't get it. Trying to get him to see what I'm saying is a fruitless endeavor. A waste of breath. Stewart's eyes narrow, but in anger. Like he's considering something.

"You want more spontaneity?" he asks.

"Yes!"

"I can be spontaneous."

Before I know it, Stewart rounds my desk and wraps me in his arms. I consider backing away, but the defiant part of me wants to see just how far he'll go. It isn't Daniel Stone bending me over my desk, but maybe, just maybe...

I gasp in alarm as his arms hug me a moment, and then he bends slightly, his arms now reaching around my waist. Stewart might be a pathologist who sits in a lab most of the day, but I know better than most that he's actually pretty athletic. He puts his muscled arms to good use as he lifts me off the ground and slings me over his shoulder.

"Stewart!" I admonish, a little louder than I

intended. "Put me down!" I try to grab onto the corner of my desk for balance. I miss and grab his ass instead.

He chortles. "This is what you wanted, Ash!"

Too late. I realize that I made a huge miscalculation by being upfront with him. Sober expression or not, Stewart is still drunk—and now he's quite literally taken my life into his hands.

"Stewart! Put me down!" I command, pounding now on his ass as he carries me out into the hallway. *No, no, no...* this can't be happening! I try to lift myself enough to shoot a glance over my shoulder to see where he's heading, but it's difficult to get my bearings bouncing on his shoulder. I think he's taking me toward the elevator. His grip tightens over the swell of my ass in response to my insistence that he put me down. At that moment, I know it's hopeless trying to negotiate with him when in such a vulnerable position. As soon as he puts me down, though, I'll make him wish he'd never...

I gulp and scramble for purchase, trying to lift myself so I can balance my hands on his hips, but I start to slip. "Stewart! I'm slipping!" The reality of being dropped prompts me to freeze. "Stewart!" My voice rising in panic now. "I'm going to fall!"

"Relax babe, I would never—"

The bastard trips. He actually *trips,* stumbling over nothing but his own impaired reflexes, and my slinky dress might as well be butter in his hands. He scrambles to catch his balance and with his body off-kilter, I slide forward. Our legs tangle. I see myself falling ass over teakettle, but I manage to instinctively twist and barely manage to break my fall with my hands, lucky I didn't break one of them in the process. I topple to the ground onto my right hip, my hands sliding forward so that I actually manage to land on my forearms. Unfortunately, Stewart slides to the side. In Stewart's defense, he twists at the last second to avoid all of his weight from crashing down on me. In *my* defense, he decides to use the front of my dress as a handhold.

A horrendous tear of fabric accompanies the sound of the elevator door *ding* and the next moment, those doors slide open. I shake Stewart's hands off me and manage to thrust myself upward onto my ass, arms braced behind me, my knees spread. I see movement and glance up.

Oh God.

Daniel Stone's grass green eyes stare down at me.

His perfect, chiseled face uncomprehending for a moment while his gaze takes in the sight. His eyes widen slightly and his eyebrows lift. Oh God. I can't speak; I can't even breathe. Of every scene in which I hoped he would find me tonight, the unfolding nightmare in which I find myself trapped never even crossed my mind.

"Mister Stone!" I gasp, struggling out from beneath Stewart. I manage to scramble to my feet with only a modicum of dignity. I'm not sure what to do, what excuses to make. "I... we were just..."

The green eyes that pin me to the spot sink lower. And lower. *Just like I imagined they would,* I consider in bewilderment, until my own gaze drops to follow his. Daniel stares at the front of my dress—or where the front of my dress *used* to be. The tastefully plunging neckline is gone; in its place is skin, skin, and more naked skin. Stewart ripped my dress all the way down to the scalloped black crest of my push-up bra.

I instinctively cross my arms to cover myself, but it's too late. I can almost see my reflection in Daniel Stone's eyes; we're standing that close. Did his pupils just dilate slightly? Am I imagining that? The look is there and gone before I can properly define what it might be.

"Excuse me," I mumble, mortified—again. I turn away and make a beeline for the women's restroom, leaving Stewart behind. As soon as the door swings shut behind me, I slide my back along the door and hunch down on the tiled floor and drop my head into my hands. Despair engulfs me. I've practically just bared my breasts in front of my crush, my *boss*. I'm humiliated, but I doubt that matters to a man like Daniel Stone. I'm going to have to face the music.

I rise and step to the sink and stare at myself in the mirror. A mess of tousled black hair and haunted brown eyes stare back at me. My pale complexion looks even more drained of color than usual, and for some reason my lipstick is smeared.

I rearrange my appearance as best I can. There's no hope for the rental dress, which I realize now I'm going to have to pay for in full. Shit. I pull the clip from my up-do and shake my hair out, then use the clip to secure my ruined dress in place. *Nice*, I grimace. The top of my bra is still visible, but this is the best I can do until I could manage to escape downstairs to the coat check. I push my way out of the restroom to find Stewart waiting for me in the hallway.

"Stewart!" I glance around, but Daniel is nowhere in sight. I don't know whether to feel relieved or disappointed by the fact. "Where is Daniel... Mister Stone?"

"He's waiting for you in your office. He wants to speak to you... alone." Stewart looks put-out. Did Daniel say something to him? Then again, Stewart is the last person I need to be worrying about right now.

Daniel Stone wants to see me? Alone? In my office? Oh God.

"Stewart, I need you to go."

Stewart looks ready to protest, until his eyes drops to the fists slowly clenching at my sides. The reality of the situation finally seems to cut through the fog of inebriation he's been swimming in.

"... all right, Ash."

"Call a cab," I say. "I'll text you tomorrow. Let's both just hope I still have a job."

He opens his mouth to say something, and by the look on his face, to apologize for being the cause of this fiasco. I don't care. I shoulder by him and walk slowly toward my office, faltering more and more with each step.

Daniel Stone is waiting for me. In my office. I'm about to be severely reprimanded, I'm sure, if not fired. What must he think of me?

At the thought of Daniel alone in my office, I stop. My hand flies to my mouth. Before Stewart carried me out the door, I left my computer open. I left my *manuscript* document open.

Oh, shit.

4

DANIEL

I wait for Ashley Shiels in her office.

The accommodations are small but serviceable. Of the three desks in the room, Ashley's desk has no personal touches. No photos, no knick-knacks, no silly mouse pads. Desktop neatly centered on her desk, its screen dark. Near one side, a laptop open. I take it all in, looking for some indication of the woman's personality, but find little evidence to lead me to a satisfying conclusion. She keeps her personal life personal, her space tidy and impersonal. An enigma, especially after what I'd just seen in the hallway.

Ashley Shiels. She's a fixture at Pen and Quill, as dependable professionally as she is beautiful. I have tried on several occasions to speak with her after I've exited my office and made my way down the hallway from my large office, but some business matter inevitably called her away. I always thought her restrained, maybe even a little uptight, but that might just be a symptom of my own presence. Most of my employees don't know how to act around me. I consider Elektra the only exception.

Nothing about Ashley was restrained just moments ago. I've barely devoted a single thought to the man that was with her since finding them both sprawled on the floor. It looked like a drunken accident, nothing more illicit than that.

But I could easily make it more illicit. I can't stop thinking about her breasts: those pert, porcelain mounds, with nothing covering them but a pair of arms and an inexpensive bra that looked as easy to tear off her as the dress she wore. I can't stop reliving the moment I saw her standing there bared before me. It was all I could do to keep from snatching her by the wrists and pulling her arms apart, the man on the floor be damned.

How dare she hide herself from me? I felt the Dom in me rising, and I've fought to tamp it down before she meets me in her office, which I know she will.

I do what I usually do in these instances, when work interferes with the pursuit of pleasure: I distract myself. There isn't much to look at here, but Ashley's laptop is open; the green light flashing rhythmically on the side. I tap the space bar and the screen lights up. I pull it toward me without much interest. Maybe I should feel guilty for invading my employee's privacy, but I doubt that a cursory glance at what she's working on—on her night off to attend the Christmas party, for that matter—will do much harm. I've already seen more of her than she was probably expecting to reveal to me.

A manuscript. I gaze at the familiar formatting. She's working on her own manuscript. Most everyone around here is secretly working on one, no surprise there. Still, I didn't expected Ashley to have a book in progress. What else is my scintillating little editorial assistant hiding from me?

"Fuck me," she begged. "Please. Any way you want me. I can't stand this torture any longer."

I lift an eyebrow. Well then.

"You've ruined your stockings," her lover purred as he swept the dark chocolate cascade of hair back from her shoulders. "You're so wet, you're positively dripping. Does my own particular brand of punishment turn you on so much?"

My cock stirs and offers an aggressive twitch at the word *punishment*. "Just what have you been writing, Ashley?" I murmur as I scroll down the page. I'm an adept speed-reader—I have to be in my line of work—but I want to take my time processing this latest revelation. Evidently, Ashley spends her spare time writing smut, and as for her predilections...

"Maybe you forgot who's boss around here," he growled as he flipped her over and shoved her back against her desk. Her pencil holder toppled and spilled its contents onto the floor, but she couldn't have put a halt to the proceedings now if she wanted to... and like hell she did want to. She let her supervisor thrust himself between her legs. She rocked her hips back against the edge of her desk. His honey-blond hair fell forward over savage green eyes, brimming with hunger for...

"Stewart! Where is Daniel... Mister Stone?"

I hear her alarmed voice coming from just outside in the hallway. It's all I can do to tear my eyes away from the screen and the torrid scene unfolding in my mind—courtesy of Ashley's sizzling-hot words. I have maybe seconds to act before she joins me.

And I do. I tab open Ashley's e-mail, attach the manuscript to my address, and hit Send. Then I close out of the window and shut the laptop, giving it a little nudge with my hand to arrange it the way I found it. There's nothing that can be done about my throbbing erection tucked against my thigh.

I watch the door, making a deal with myself as I wait for her to enter. It's something I'm used to doing, but this time the deal is unusually sweet. If Ashley Shiels walks in here with the front of her dress torn, I intend to do something about it. Something that is decidedly *not* chivalrous.

She pushes the door open, and I'm disappointed, though not surprised. I knew she was smart enough to engineer a quick fix, and she's managed to salvage the shredded fabric and make herself halfway presentable again in the process.

Pity.

"Miss Shiels." I keep my voice low, though I'm already certain of our privacy. I motion toward the door, and she nods, closing it quietly behind her.

"I..." she begins. Her eyes flicker to her laptop. I see a look of puzzlement. She probably remembers leaving her laptop open, but I allow her to second-guess her own memory.

"Please." I indicate the chair sitting catty-corner to her desk. She sits without a word. I need her to see me as her superior, now more than ever. "I just wanted to make sure you were all right." I try to establish eye contact, but it's difficult when she's obviously determined to look everywhere *but* directly at me.

"Yes. I'm all right... thank you for asking, Mister Stone."

Her cheeks flush a deep, fetching rose, and I imagine she's reliving the moment. I hoped she would. A part of me hopes the way I'm looked at her registered.

"Please. Call me Daniel."

"I don't know what you must think of me," she stutters. "But I'm not... I wasn't..."

"That man. Is he your boyfriend?"

"No."

The refutation is so immediate and flatly spoken that I can't help snorting with laughter. Her dark lashes sweep against her cheeks as her gaze falls to her lap, and her blush deepens. I've known women who flush all the way down to the tops of their breasts. Is Ashley one of them? Unfortunately, her ingenuity with the dress prevents me from finding out.

"Was he harassing you?"

"He's... no. Stewart's a friend," Ashley replies. "He had a little too much to drink. That's all."

"Then it's a good thing I called a cab for him."

She nods gratefully, the buoyant raven waves of her hair bouncing against her cheeks. There's a thought itching at the back of my mind, but I'll have to wait until I'm home—with her manuscript in my hand—to explore it further.

Just where do you find your inspiration, Ashley?

"I know you have a lot on your plate right now," I continue. "I wanted to take this moment to personally thank you for your work on the Christmas party. I knew we were in good hands when Elektra said she delegated to you."

"It's... it was nothing." She shakes her head, but perks up a little. "Did you get a chance to go to the party?"

"I don't usually enjoy these things."

"Oh."

"Not *usually*," I emphasize before she has a chance to be disappointed. I want that blush back. I want more than that. I rise from behind her desk, and she quickly pushes out from her chair to follow my lead—like an indentured servant who follows the Master's lead. "But tonight has been... illuminating. You're a hard worker, Miss Shiels."

"Thank you, Mister Stone... Daniel." She struggles with my first name now, but not, I noticed, in front of the drunken 'friend' she left back in the hallway.

"Is there anything else I can assist you with this evening?"

"Not this evening, no. But I'm glad you asked." I move around the desk to stand closer to her. She doesn't shrink from me—which is a welcome relief from my conversations with some of the other editorial assistants this evening—but I entertain the idea that she feels the heat radiating between us all the same. I'm still hard, but her eyes never so much as glance away from my face. *Good.* "I might have a special job for you. Nothing that will interfere with your work assisting Elektra... but we don't need to discuss it tonight."

I let my eyes drop, allowing her to feel the full weight of my gaze trained on those already-heavy breasts of hers. I betray nothing: no disproval, no lasciviousness. I want her to recall this moment and wonder at its meaning when she lies alone tonight.

"Come by my office first thing Monday morning, and we'll discuss the details," I say. "Good night, Miss Shiels."

"Good night, Daniel."

She backs out of my way to allow me to pass, and it's all I can do to not crowd her into the deeper shadows of her office and ask her to give me a hand with the aroused state for which she is wholly responsible. Something tells me that Ashley would prefer it if I *didn't* ask.

I nod, hold her eyes a moment longer, then slip past her and let myself out the door. I contemplate all the ways I'm going to get Ashley Shiels out of my system on the long elevator ride down to the parking garage.

Monday can't come soon enough. In the meantime, I've got a book to read.

5

ASHLEY

I walk into work Monday morning with every expectation of being fired.

I'm going to go about it gracefully, I've decided. I spent all weekend working out how my departure will go. Tory will cry into my commemorative Disney mug that I will graciously gift her, and Elektra will look on with disapproval as I gather my sparse belongings up in the cardboard box that I will soon be living out of.

Oh, shit. I forgot the box in my car.

I keep walking, although I can't help slowing my pace as I near my office. I can't help remembering how I found Daniel there the night of the Christmas party. I am absolutely positive that I left my laptop open when Stewart carried me out of the room—and I'm positive that Daniel must have seen my manuscript. Just thinking about that cool gaze of his reading over my hot, illicit fantasies is enough to confirm what I already suspect: by the end of today, I'm going to be out of a job. The fiasco with Stewart might have been forgivable as an accident, but there's nothing accidental about what I wrote in my novel. He's got to think by now that I'm some kind of sexual deviant, and worst of all, there's the chance he recognized some of his own traits, purloined and penned into the character of my male lead.

But I'm still kidding myself. It isn't just 'some' of Daniels' characteristics I used to inform my novel's hero; it's *all* of them.

I drop my purse onto my desk, hang my coat on the back of my chair, and look around desperately for something that might occupy my attention. I'm early to work; there were no other cars in the garage.

Daniel doesn't always park his Rolls Royce in the company garage. When I asked the valet posted up at the front entrance of the building if Mister Stone was already in, he answered: "Oh, yes. Mister Stone has been here for an hour at least already."

I'm so fucked.

I take a moment alone in my office to straighten my blouse and smooth my skirt. I compose myself to the best of my ability. I even dig around in my purse for my compact, only to discover the screen lit up on my phone. I glance at it and see a series of text messages from Stewart.

Stewart: Hey, babe. Everything okay?

Stewart: I didn't hear from you all weekend. Figured you were still pissed about the dress.

Stewart: If you need help paying for the damage, you know I'll be good for it in about a month or so.

Stewart: I still want to talk about us. Call me when you can. ;)

No apology about what happened, but I didn't really expect one. Still, it would be nice if Stewart realizes on his own that my latest radio silence is, and has never been, about the dress. I'm still furious with him for showing up drunk to an event that he *knew* was important to me. Not only that—I didn't even invite him to begin with! He must have heard about it from Tory.

Well, at least there are no more potentially embarrassing work parties in my future. That's about the only silver lining to all this that I can come up with.

I finally square my shoulders and venture down the hallway to Daniel's office. I knock on the door. I hear a faint 'come in' and enter.

"Shut the door behind you please, and sit down." He gestures to the plush leather chair in front of his massive desk.

I do as he asks. No sooner than I sit down than he gets down to business, but the business he begins to discuss is not what I imagined.

"Your characters are relatable. There's almost something familiar about them."

His words raise every hair on my body. Confirmation. He read my manuscript. My mouth feels dry. My heart pounds violently. Any moment now the other shoe is going to drop. Any moment now. "Yes, well," I stammer. "I try to write characters as if they're people, since it's people who will be reading and relating to my characters."

I cringe. If this is my elevator pitch, it's already off the cables. I try to summon the right words and start over. "I especially think it's important to make them relatable... or as you put it, *familiar...* considering... well. Considering."

"Especially considering the subject matter," Daniel offers.

I nod in agreement. What can I say?

"I don't need to tell you that bondage fiction is a niche, Miss Shiels. A very *profitable* niche, especially for a writer with your talent."

A blush warms my cheeks. I look up at him as he rises from his desk and crosses to look out his floor-to-ceiling window. Of all the words he could have used to describe me, 'talented' is the last one I expected.

"... but it's a niche that suffers from a lack of accessibility," he continues. "I find your manuscript very accessible."

"Thank you." I want to ask him if he's finished reading it all the way through, but I hold my tongue. "I... that means a lot coming from you."

"I know."

He turns from the window to look me directly in the eyes once more. I force myself to hold his gaze.

"Miss Shiels, I didn't invite you up to my office to compliment you. I want Pen and Quill to publish your book."

My jaw drops. I pull myself together and curtail my emotions. Oh, but it's so hard. He wants to publish my book? How—he leans against the window and crosses his arms over his chest, studying my reaction with just the hint of a smile.

"Is that a 'yes'?"

I nod.

"You know you aren't beholden to what I want just because I'm the CEO. You may work for me, but what you write is yours and yours alone. All I'm offering you is a platform and the opportunity to publish with the biggest independent company in the country."

"And would you advise me to turn down that opportunity?" I ask him, recovering with admirable confidence, if I do say so myself.

"There's more to my terms. I want to personally represent you."

My heart skips a beat. "But if... say my book *is* a success." Just thinking it is was exhilarating, let alone saying it out loud. "Say I decide to become an author full-time. You'll lose an editorial assistant."

"I'll lose a damn good one," he agrees. "But hopefully I'll have gained a client. One eager to continue repeating her successes."

"If my book is a success."

"I don't think you understand what you're sitting on, Miss Shiels."

He pushes himself away from the window and walks behind my chair. I try to follow him with my eyes, but wind up facing forward as he pauses directly behind my chair. His hands come to a rest on my shoulders, so close the knuckles of each thumb brush against the skin of my neck. I barely quell an excited shudder.

Is he trying to seduce me? That's what my intrepid heroine would ask, but I can't bring myself to form the question.

"No. You don't understand." Daniel crouches down behind my chair and his voice drops to an almost-whisper. "But you will."

I shiver as his breath warms the back of my neck. "I'm sorry?"

"You're a talented editorial assistant, Miss, Shiels, and it shows through your writing."

He withdraws his hands and moves to my side. I sink back into the chair, heart pounding in my chest.

"But there are still places in the book where your research falls short," Daniel concludes as he sits down in his chair.

I study him, not sure what he's getting at. "Such as?"

He grins. "A few scenes come to mind."

I find it difficult to swallow. Judging by his expression, I think I know exactly the scenes he means. I'm certainly not going to argue that I have any firsthand knowledge of the bondage lifestyle. His next words could knock me over with a feather.

"I want you to have lunch with me tomorrow."

"I'm sorry?" I ask. Obviously, it's not the response I intend, but the only one I can manage at this point. I'm sure I mishear him... or maybe my lust-addled brain fails to compute his request the way he means it.

Daniel looks faintly annoyed at having to repeat himself, but I swear, there's an amused twist to his normally reserved smile that I've never seen before.

"I said, would you like to have lunch with me tomorrow, Miss Shiels?"

That's not what you said at all, I realize. The first version of his invitation wasn't an invitation: it was a command. A thrill of excitement shudders through me. It's probably just my imagination... Anyway, Daniel is doubtless used to giving orders, considering he's the CEO. It's probably second nature for him to frame his invite that way.

"I'm sorry..." I clear my throat. "Yes, of course, I would love to have lunch with you tomorrow, Daniel. Mister Stone... Daniel." Why does every version of his name suddenly sound like an intimacy I haven't earned yet? I blame the way he's looking at me. There's no way a girl can hope to feel platonic *or* professional with those gorgeous green eyes of his fixed on her. I wish my body didn't interpret his look as a signal to get so aroused. Already I can feel heat between my legs, kindling to a slow burn. One prolonged glance between us and I'm wetter than Stewart's clinical fumbling has ever managed.

"Good," he says. "I look forward to it."

I want to kick myself. His reply is perfectly formal —mine, on the other hand, definitely employs the use of the L-word. I nod quickly and rise, heading for the door before I can say something that will—

"Oh, and Miss Shiels?"

I turn, foolish heart leaping into my throat. He smiles, wide and brilliant and beautiful, and I know I could die happy on my way out the door knowing *that* mouth, belonging to *that* man, invited *me* to lunch. Never mind that he wants to represent my novel.

"Yes?" Basic manners find a way to slip past my frantically beating heart.

"I'll send a new dress over to you." Daniel is already making himself busy with some documents he's pulled from his desk drawer. "Is your office all right for the delivery?"

I have no words. I'm a romance writer, working in a premier publishing house, and I can't find a damn word in any language to convey my assent. I nod again, and turn to escape before I find a new way to make a fool of myself.

Those at least I seem to know in abundance.

6

DANIEL

I'm rather surprised by how much I'm actually looking forward to having lunch with Ashley. She'll be here any minute. I've never particularly been interested in the private lives of the people working for me at Pen & Quill. I'm also forced to admit to myself that if I didn't find her laptop open on her desk, nor been curious enough to look at the screen to read that snippet of the manuscript, I might never have noticed her at all—beyond her work, that is.

What does that say about me?

Nevertheless, I did see that snippet, and I finished reading the entire manuscript following the party. And yes, it definitely kept me up until dawn—mentally and physically. By the time I read a mere five pages or so through the manuscript, I made the connection. Ashley's male character was definitely fashioned after me, and her female character was easily identifiable as

Ashley herself. A common newbie mistake, but in this case amusing and quite titillating.

It didn't make me angry or offended; rather, I felt flattered. As I continued to read, I sometimes felt amused. Did I really appear that way to other people? Or was it just Ashley, who I was realizing had more than a mild crush on me. More like lust. She lusted after me... or at least the character in the book. Most of all, it turned me on. Who knew? Not only the witty dialogue and interplay between the characters, but their sex. Hot, passionate, different.

I don't know how many times as I read the manuscript that I stopped reading, closed my eyes, and pictured Ashley's somewhat shy, more than capable, office-persona professionalism and demure personality in a new light. What was she hiding beneath the surface of that calm veneer? She was one of our best editorial assistants, more than capable of overseeing other assistants. But Ashley the author was so much more... developed. She wasn't merely fixing other authors' grammar or syntax or prose. No, this Ashley is passionate, intriguing, and offers an endearing, somewhat naïve, yet sexually adventurous character personified in the pages of her manuscript.

Wishful thinking on her part, or her true persona? Is she really such a tigress in the sack? I imagine her with that guy who was with her at the party and shake my head. No way. Still, it's a question that intrigues me and piques my curiosity in more ways than one. I want to discover the answer to that question myself, but that also triggers a new issue. That invisible yet necessary line between employers and employees. How do I get around that?

FINALLY, I decide to just throw my suggestion out there and see what happens. Of course, I will emphasize that her job will be safe regardless of her answer. She can always say no. She doesn't know me, not really, and I don't know that much about her, so the trust level isn't there, but I'll just have to wait and see. Still, thinking about Ashley and her writing, especially the sex scenes she described, I have a feeling that she will go for it. Because she obviously has a crush on me, I don't feel like I'm particularly taking advantage; rather, I'm making myself available to her.

I also need to assure her that I still want to publish her manuscript even if she doesn't want to have sex with me. Sure, it needs some tweaking, but it's good stuff. Really good stuff. I don't think she will turn down an opportunity to explore in greater depth exactly what's involved in the relationship of a Dom/submissive. She has to know the author's mantras: Write what you know. Show, don't tell. If she's going to write about it, she has to have accurate details, and to be frank, there are several instances in her manuscript that lack... flavor. What better way to hone her writing skills, especially in this niche, than learning by doing?

She'll go for that, won't she? At least the character in her book would. Another thing to consider is the subject matter of her book. I have no idea regarding her sexual preferences, but anybody who can write hot, über-detailed scenes like she did, enough to get me hot and aroused, has to know what they're talking about, and if the opportunity arises, no pun intended, I'm more than willing to take advantage.

I'm already seated at the table I reserved in a corner of the restaurant where we will have the opportunity to speak more privately. While I'm expecting her, when she walks through the door, it's if I'm seeing her for the first time. I am, really, in spite of the fact that she's worked for me for quite a while. She doesn't have her hair pulled into the long ponytail she usually wears at the office. Her wavy black hair hangs loose around her shoulders, tendrils draping her face. The effect doesn't appear to be deliberate, nor an attempt on her part to be seductive, which it is. The look is more that of a woman rushing to get where she needed to be. I smile. She looks like a breath of fresh air. So cliché, I know, but it feels like that. Here is a woman who isn't out to impress, doesn't put on false airs, doesn't have to work hard at conveying her sexual appeal. I notice again how tall she is, how perfect her proportions. Why haven't I ever seen her before?

I'm certainly not one to ignore pretty women but somehow, Ashley has escaped my radar. Until now. She pauses inside the door and speaks to the hostess, who gestures in my direction as she escorts her to my table. As she approaches, I rise and wait for her to slide into the booth seat across from me before sitting down. She smiles nervously, but then again, not unexpected. I am her boss after all.

"Your server will be here in just a moment," the hostess points at the leather-bound menu at each place setting. "Can I get you something to drink? A cocktail? Coffee?"

Ashley's reply startles me.

"Can I have a diet cola please, extra ice?"

I nod and glance up at the hostess. "Two diet colas, extra ice please."

The hostess nods and quickly walks away while Ashley looks at me and smiles.

"I never imagined you as a diet soda person. Scotch perhaps, maybe gin, but not diet cola."

I offer an easy shrug. "The purpose of our lunch today is to get to know one another a little more, actually. After all, if we're going to do this, we have to be comfortable with each other, right?"

She nods.

I continue. "I want to know your likes and dislikes." I have her attention. "My intention is to imply more than just your choice of drink. If we're going to do this, I need to make sure that we're compatible. I want to know what makes you tick. What makes you hum, what you enjoy drinking and eating, and then comes the sex." I pause and give her one of my best stern looks. "Nothing worse than entering this kind of a relationship and having things go downhill fast."

Before she can reply, a server arrives, places to tall glasses of diet cola bubbling with carbonation in front of each of us, setting straws on the table next to the glasses. "Would you like a few minutes to look over the menu before ordering?"

I shake my head. Time to display some control. "I'm ready to order." I glance at Ashley, who stares at me, one eyebrow slightly lifted. "Two small spinach salads, the works, with balsamic vinaigrette dressing on the side. For the entrée, pork medallions, brown rice, and asparagus."

The server glances at Ashley, but she's still looking at me. She offers a slight nod and the server turns and walks away. I continue speaking. "In our new... relationship, it's important that we set the stage. I'm the one in control. You're not."

A slight flash of alarm, eyes wide, mouth slightly open, but she quickly brings her reaction under control in a matter of seconds. "Speak your mind, actually."

"I'm just... I didn't realize that it's starting already."

She fidgets with her straw but doesn't pull it from its paper case. She's nervous, no doubt about it. Another reason why I've taken the lead quickly. "I want to reiterate, Ashley, that no matter what happens, there will be no repercussions if you decide to back out. At any time. That being said, I certainly hope that you'll take me up on my offer. After all, I can give you a very intimate look at the kind of lifestyle you describe in your book. You know the saying, right?"

"Write what you know," she says softly.

I grin. "Exactly." I adjust my napkin and the

polished silverware atop it, trying not to stare but finding it difficult to keep my eyes off of her. "First, I want you to feel comfortable with me. Once we agree to this... relationship, not only will I be your boss, but I'll be your lover, your Dom. But I want you to know that at work, those lines will not be crossed. At work, I'm your boss. Nothing more, nothing less. Outside of work..."

"I.... I understand."

I say nothing more as the server brings our salads and entrées. The salad dressing is in a small porcelain curette. I watch as she doles out a slow, trickling stream of the dressing onto her salad. Her hand trembles and she refuses to look at me. Okay, slight detour.

"So, Ashley, tell me about yourself."

She glances up, startled, hand frozen in the air. "There's really not much to tell," she finally says. "I've been working at—"

"No," I say, shaking my head. She place the porcelain curette back on the table. I extend my hand and place it over her wrist. Her skin feels soft and warm. For the first time, I notice that she keeps her fingernails shorter than most, and her fingers look strong, capable... I force my thoughts away from how those hands will feel wrapped around my dick. I give her arm a squeeze. "Tell me about you. Where did you come from? Who are your people?"

"My people... well, I grew up in Brooklyn," she begins. "Um, well, I have two parents, but they got divorced when I was about ten. An amenable divorce," she clarifies, poking at her salad. "My dad got an apartment not too far from where we lived, so me and my younger brother, Andrew, spent plenty of time with each parent. He lives across the river in New Jersey now with his girlfriend. We get together on holidays, a good thing, but other than that, we don't see each other very often."

She pauses and stabs a few leaves of spinach onto her fork and lifts it to her mouth. I watch, not just because I find her nervousness adorable, but I want to see how she feels about being watched. Watching is a big part of our new relationship. This might just seem like a getting-to-know-you lunch as far as she is concerned, but for me, it offers a glimpse into what I might expect from her.

"Where do you want to go from here?"

She chews quickly, swallows, and then looks at me, touching her index finger to the corner of her lip. A self-conscious gesture.

"I went to NYU to study journalism—"

"No, Ashley. I mean, what is it you want out of life?"

I can tell that the abrupt change in topic from her background to asking about her dreams, goals, aspirations of life startled her. So far though, she's responding like a person would during a job interview. I don't want that. I want her to tell me what she thinks, feels, and believes in. How long will it take her to understand that? She recovers quickly. She places her fork on her napkin and looks me straight in the eye.

"I have no idea," she replies, offering a tiny shrug,

another indication of her personality. "What everyone wants, I suppose. To earn a living, make enough money to get by, to be happy with my job, to find myself in a solid relationship... what about you?"

I grin. That's what I wanted to see. I respond to her query. "Well, I'm an only child. My dad comes from old money, New York money, and he married a woman half his age, and after several tries, well, there I was. My father died when I was three-years-old, so I never really knew him." I take a sip of my cola and then continue. "My mother is overprotective, almost excessively so. I'm a type A personality, obviously, and I graduated from Yale with an MBA."

Ashley nods, cuts one of her pork medallions into small pieces, stabs at piece with her fork and lifts it to her mouth, chewing thoughtfully. "Why did you go into publishing?"

Interesting question. I also take a bite of pork, matching my movements to hers without breaking eye contact. She doesn't either. Very good. Very good indeed. "After two years working at my family's company, import-exports, I knew that wasn't exactly what I wanted. I went back to school, got a bachelor's degree in comparative literature, and then I started Pen and Quill."

She laughs softly. "And what did your family have to say about that?

I grin. "My mom freaked. But we compromised. I'm still the CEO of our family business, but I delegate. What I enjoy most is the publishing industry."

She nods, seemingly now at a loss for words. "And you, Ashley. You're gifted as an editor. I appreciate your work. But why do you want to become an author, and why erotica? More specifically, why this niche of erotica?"

I watch as a blush travels all the way from the base of her neck up into her cheeks. Still, she doesn't flinch.

"This is kind of personal, but—"

"Actually, if I have my way, after lunch, we're going to go upstairs and get naked together. How much more personal can you get?" Her blush deepens, the pulse in her neck throbbing. Is she game or will she cut and run? I hope for the former, because the more time I spend with her, the more attracted I am to her. I enjoy sex, and while I appreciate beauty as much as the next guy, I don't place as much importance on looks as I do, well, how to say it politely? Enthusiasm between the sheets? The urge to push the envelope? Many of my partners were okay, in a traditional sense as far as sex is concerned. Of course, I have some like Crystal who indulge like me, and with whom I feel I can be who I want to be. Still, I've never found a partner that I feel... trite as it sounds—complete with. One who can match my appetite, one who is totally in tune with me, my rhythms, my needs, my desire to experience total unity.

I've always been good at sex, but after so many years, it just seemed routine. After a while, it just got boring. That's what attracted me to the world of BDSM. But what about Ashley?

"Well, I've never really..." she pauses, takes another bite of pork, chews and swallows, then follows that with a long sip of her cola.

I watch. She clears her throat, darts a glance down at her plate, then up, this time not breaking eye contact. She straightens her shoulders.

"I've had a few boyfriends over the years," she admits. "I lost my virginity when I was seventeen, with a guy I'd been dating for about a year. After that, it didn't seem like such a big deal anymore, as long as the guys were protected."

She pauses, lifts an eyebrow in question, and when I nod in understanding, she continues.

"I've had a handful of flings, but none of them lasted very long... anywhere from a weekend to a couple of weeks."

"Why?"

"Why what?"

"Why just flings? I would expect someone with a solid head on her shoulders to be more demanding, to want a long-term relationship."

She swallows. "Well, none of them turned out to be what I was looking for."

I'm intrigued by another ensuing flush of color darkening her cheeks before she continues.

"I like sex, don't get me wrong, but to be frank, I could live without it."

I grin. "That's because you haven't met the right partner yet."

She almost makes a face. Almost.

"I'm currently in an on-again off-again relationship with Stewart... the guy you met by the elevator, but it's more of a friends-with-benefits thing." She pauses. "At least on my end. He thinks he wants to marry me."

"And you don't?"

She shakes her head. "Stewart's a good guy, but he's just... he's just not the one."

"So, what do you feel is missing? From these relationships?"

Her eyes lock with mine again. "I'm not quite sure how to explain it. Maybe my ideas of sex and passion and excitement are just a childhood fantasy, but I thought it would be, well, more special." She shakes her head. "I'm not making myself clear. It's hard to explain."

"Not really," I say, placing my fork on my plate. Neither of us have eaten much, but I now have a greater understanding of what makes Ashley tick. She's looking for some excitement, something different, something to ignite a deep sense of thrill that she can't even identify. Passion that she longs for. A deeper connection, not only in a sexual relationship, but between her and her partner. I have no doubt that I'm the man who can do that.

"Well here it is, Ashley, in plain English. Take me up on my offer and I'll show you what you're missing. But first, we need to make sure that we're sexually compatible and that you'll be comfortable with this world." I wipe my mouth with my cloth napkin and offer a small shrug. "If you want to write erotica, about bondage, about domination, you have to understand what it's all about. You can't just read about it. You have to live it. You have to feel it. You have to experience it."

I reach into my pocket, extract my wallet, and place several bills on the pristine white tablecloth. I stand and hold out my hand. She looks up at me and for a few seconds, and I think she might change her mind, but to my pleasure, she lifts her hand and places it in mine.

"All right then." I smile. "Let's go."

7

ASHLEY

I 'm freaking. *What's the matter with you? What do you think you're doing? This is going to ruin everything!*

I've always admired Daniel, it isn't that. He gets my engines revving. I've been fantasizing about him for a long, long time. But this could end badly. Fantasies were just that. I don't really know anything about the kind of man he is. At work, yes, sort of. Out of work? No clue. He could be an arrogant bastard. He could be lame in bed. He could be twisted, as in the I'm-going-to-cause-you-pain kind of twisted. I'm looking for something exciting in the bedroom, but I don't necessarily want pain. A pinch here, a slap on the ass there is okay, but nothing truly painful. I want to enjoy the sex too, not just endure it.

I've also heard the rumors. Office gossip. He's often seen about town with a different woman on his arm every night. How in the world am I going to compete with them? The women he goes out with—again gossip—are the hoity-toity type. Socially aware, known in their circles, attached to boardrooms or high-power positions. Does he do... does he have regular sex with them or are they all into the bondage scene? I scoff. What difference does it make?

I'm here now. Me. I'm going to dip my toe into the waters and see what happens. He promises nothing, except that I will still have my job and he'll still publish my book. If things don't work out like I expect, things will just go back to the way they've been.

Won't they?

I know nothing about the world of bondage. Sure, I've read about some of it, but reading and doing are two different things. I imagine myself handcuffed to a bedframe with pink, fuzzy, padded handcuffs, and him having his way with me.

No doubt about it, that image gets me hot. Just the thought of it has my nipples tingling and hardening and my pussy clenching with anticipation. At the same time, I know that I'm no match in sexual prowess nor as experienced as Daniel. I know that he can please me, but what if I don't please him? Can I please a man like him? Self-doubt creeps in. I'll be mortified if I don't.

No, I'm making a mistake. I'm leaving myself open to ridicule, to—

"Don't be nervous," he says as he guides me out of

the restaurant and down the short hallway toward the elevators. He planned it this way. A light lunch in the restaurant of the Westin Hotel. A room already reserved upstairs for our rendezvous. I can't help my vivid imagination from running amok. I fantasize him emerging from the bathroom wearing a pair of leather chaps, holding a short whip or something. God, how cliché is that? No, no he wouldn't do that, he isn't the type.

Is he?

Anything I know about bondage I've read about in other books, other romance novels. At the moment, more than any other time in my life, I feel like a fraud. Embarrassed, I stand next to him in the elevator, the scent of his cologne or aftershave, whatever it is, wafting toward me. He smells good. He always does. He holds my hand; warm, strong, offering a sense of security and comfort.

I might as well just fess up. I look up at him, watching as he watches the numbers of the floors we pass light up in fluorescent green. "Daniel, I should tell you..." He glances away from the numbers and looks down at me, giving me his full attention. "I'm probably not as experienced as... no, that isn't right." I shake my head, along with an eye roll. "I'm not as experienced as some of the other women you've been with, so—"

"Relax, Ashley," he says. "That's what this is all about, isn't it? You want to learn?"

I nod.

"I'll be your teacher. I'll show you. But first, we just need to become acquainted with one another in a more carnal sense. You just need to trust me, all right?"

I nod and say nothing more as the elevator continues to rise until it finally stops on the top floor. A penthouse suite? The elevator doors ding open and, still holding my hand, he guides me out into the carpeted hallway. I walk beside him toward a door a short distance down the hall. I swallow, then laugh at myself. Why the dread? You're not being led to the gallows!

He pulls a key card from his inner jacket pocket. My heart pounds. I hope my hand isn't clammy. I stare down at our joined hands; his large, firm, and browned by at least part of his life lived outdoors, mine smaller and pale.

The green lights of the electronic door lock flash, and he pushes down on the handle and opens the door. He let's go of my hand and braces it against the door over my head, gesturing for me to enter in front of him. Despite my nervousness, despite my urge to suddenly turn and run, I do, and then pause in the small foyer, forcing myself to be brave. I want this, don't I? I've admired Daniel from afar for so long, and now here I am, about to have sex with him in a pent-house suite of one of the nicest hotels in the city.

"Make yourself comfortable," he says.

Heavy curtains are pulled back from an expansive and gorgeous view of the city through a floor-to-ceiling window. A filmy white curtain pulled halfway across the massive window allows a sense of privacy and bathes the room in a comforting glow. I pause, taking it all in; the plush carpet, freshly vacuumed, the sunken living room, resplendently furnished with not one, but two beige leather sofas, two arm chairs at opposite ends of a maple coffee table, and beyond that, the wet bar in the corner between the edge of the window and a hallway that certainly leads to the—

"Would you like a drink?"

A buzz might be nice, consider it, but then change my mind. Good or bad, I want to remember every second of what is about to happen. I don't want my thoughts dulled with booze. "No thank you." I step toward the windows, staring at the buildings that fill the horizon until, in the distance, I find the interstate, cars streaming along like a slithering snake, and beyond that, a brief glimpse of the harbor.

I hear movement behind me, then feel his hands on my shoulders. "It's beautiful, isn't it?" I feel the need to fill the silence. I briefly close my eyes and tell myself to relax.

"It is," he agrees.

He turns me so that I face him. My breasts press against his chest, standing so close that my chin brushes against his shirt as I tilt my head to look up at him. I'm a tall girl, and Daniel, standing at six-feet-two, is only about six inches taller than me. Our eyes lock and I find it difficult to look away. Those light greenish-blue eyes of his, the way they look at mine, have me frozen like a deer in the headlights.

He glances down at my mouth, and my nipples harden. I barely squelch the gasp that rises in my throat. Such heat, such promise... a small smile plays about his lips.

"You're nervous."

He sees it, so I can't lie. I nod. He lifts a hand and cups it around my jaw, his thumb tracing the skin of my cheek under my eye. His index finger traces the line of my nose, and then along the bottom of my lip. I barely hold back a shiver. How long have I wanted this? How many times have I been in bed with Stewart, wishing that the man rocking his hips above me was Daniel? I'm excited, anxious, and filled with trepidation all at the same time. What if I don't please him? What if—

He takes my hand and leads me down a short hallway, pausing only long enough to allow me to enter the bedroom before him. If I wasn't so nervous, I would've been more dismayed by the opulence. A massive, king-sized bed with a plump maroon comforter, white pillowcases stark in contrast. At least eight pillows, plump and carefully arranged at the head of the bed. On either side of that bed stands two small end tables, maple like the coffee table in the living area, with Tiffany lamps. As with the main room, a glass, floor-to-ceiling window looks out onto the city, but as with the living room, a filmy white curtain is completely drawn over the glass, offering more privacy.

On the wall to the left stands a bank of rolling glass closet doors. The bed and end tables take up the other wall, and opposite that stands a dresser, a built-in niche with shelves and a huge flat-screen TV, and beside that, through a half-open door, is the bathroom.

Now's your chance to change your mind... The idea reverberates around my head. This is crazy. Risky. Yes, I've crushed on Daniel ever since I first started at the Pen and Quill. Yes, I always wanted something more in my sex life, although I couldn't quite identify what that implied. It was only after I started editing some of the novels submitted for publication that I learned about the world of bondage. Only then did I realize there was so much more. Only then did I discover that Daniel obviously knew a great deal about that world based on his comments on my edits before we went to press.

My heart pounds. I can't help feeling nervous. What if my body doesn't appeal to him? What if I don't please him? What if—

He grasps my hand again and guides me toward the bed. He sits down, gently tugging me down as well. I sit next to him, focused on our intertwined fingers.

"This is just us getting to know each other, Ashley. No pressure, okay?"

I'm glad we're just going to have normal sex first, which might help me feel more comfortable around him. I shouldn't expect myself to be an expert in this. He shouldn't either. I also have to think of him as just a man, a handsome, desirable man. Not my boss. I can't think about having sex with my boss. That is just too...

complicated. I also can't start freaking out about a world that I only read about, one that I barely have a grasp on, one that I barely understand, and expect myself to know—

"First, a few rules."

His comment startles me from my thoughts. "Rules?"

He nods. "The world of dominance and submission is not a free-for-all, Ashley. It's not about inflicting pain. It's not about making you do something you don't want to do." He pauses. "Of course, in this relationship, I am the Master or the Dom. You, likewise, will be the sub, sometimes called the slave."

I knew that much.

"But in order for us to be completely successful in this Dom/sub relationship, we also have to be able—and willing—to communicate. To feel free and safe, expressing our feelings and our desires." He pauses again. "Do you understand?"

I nod. Already I'm learning something new. This type of relationship is supposed to be satisfying for both partners, not just a person taking on the Master role and having his or her way with the other participant. He's also suggesting that we have to be compatible; that we have to have an affinity for one another.

"In order to be successful and create a full and satisfying relationship for both of us, we both have to have goals, and our goals should be one and the same."

"All right," I say. "So, what is your goal?"

"That both of us gain pleasure from the experience."

I nod. "I want that, too." I mean it, but I'm also slightly afraid. In some of the books I've read, the interactions seemed relatively one-sided, sometimes venturing into cruelty and dissatisfaction. With Daniel, I want to—

"Mutual enjoyment of both partners in the Dom/sub relationship is the goal. Neither has all the power, and neither gives up complete control. Remember that." He stands and removes his jacket, placing it carefully over the back of a chair near the end table.

My heart trip-hammers as I watch. This is happening. It's happening now.

"Whether it's with me or someone else, it's important to understand your role as a sub, but at the same time, never to give up all control over the situation."

My eyes are riveted to his fingers, and I watch as he begins to unbutton his shirt. Beneath the starched white of his dress shirt I see a glimpse of hard, muscular chest, hairless. When he yanks his shirt from his trousers, I barely hold back a gasp of surprise. He's beautifully formed, his muscular definition much deeper, more apparent than I ever imagined. I feel an immediate surge of desire contracting my pussy.

"Take off your blouse."

Startled by the command, I hesitate. Embarrassed and self-conscious. But this is what I want, right? I feel a flush rise in my cheeks, but I try not to show outward emotion. Slowly, nervously, I unbutton my blouse and allow my blouse to slide off my shoulders onto the bedspread, watching as his eyes focus on my breasts, covered only by the black lacy Victoria's Secret bra that I spent half of my grocery money on yesterday.

I sit straight, resisting the urge to cover my breasts with my hands from his unwavering gaze. Instead, I place them on either side of me on the bedspread, my fingers clutching the plush fullness of the maroon fabric.

He slowly unbuckles his belt as he continues. "Neither one of us is to initiate any action that causes injury. Neither to our bodies, nor toward our mental and emotional comfort levels. We will discuss our boundaries before we proceed deeper into the Dom/sub relationship. You understand?"

"Yes," I barely manage to choke out, my gaze riveted to the bulge behind his zipper. He unzips his pants. I can barely breathe.

"Pain is acceptable, as long as it provides pleasure, although sometimes it can be used to correct behaviors. Nevertheless, pain is not the foundation of this relationship. Do you understand?"

I yank my gaze from his crotch and look up at him, gazing intently down at me. I nod, then swallow as he shrugs off his shoes and allows his pants to slip down and pool around his ankles. I feel an almost electrical charge surge from behind my breasts down my spine, warming my belly, and causing a growing heat in my own groin.

"We will make pre-agreed-upon limits, specifying what is acceptable and what is not. Boundaries. These boundaries are not to be crossed unless discussed beforehand, and the boundaries don't change unless we both agree to them. Do you understand?"

I try to focus. Really I do, but oh my God, he's so much more than I ever expected. His voice is low, soothing, like a teacher, but all I can focus on is that broad chest, those muscular abs, his narrow hips, and his rock-hard legs. At the junction of those legs, his obvious arousal, pressing against his... not exactly the traditional boxers that I remember my brother wearing around the house, but not those tighty-whities, either.

He sits down on the bed next to me, warmth emanating from his skin. He smells wonderful, sexy, like a man. He wraps his arms around me and pulls me backward onto the bed, facing each other. His hands begin to work at the button of my pants. Every part of my body begins to throb with desire and anticipation. I struggle to catch my breath, not sure exactly what to do with my hands as he continues to talk to me, explaining these rules, as if I'm not lying practically naked next to him.

He lay right in front of me, his hand on my hip, his mouth so close I feel his breath on my cheek as he speaks, my hands clutch in front of my breasts, not sure what to do with them.

"We'll have to come up with a safeword for you, something that you can say that will stop any action. Safewords are important, but are not typically needed if the Dom and the sub understand one another in regard to their desires and limitations."

His fingers ease under the waistline of my pants and begin tugging downward. I lift my hips slightly off the bed to facilitate their removal. His voice purrs.

"Remember, Ashley, communication is essential."

He pauses, his fingers now tugging on the strap of my thong. "So, tell me, Ashley, tell me what you want."

What do I want? I want to feel his lips on mine. I want to feel his tongue in my mouth. I want to feel his mouth encompassing my nipple, suckling. I want to feel his rock-hard cock inside me, surging, my legs spread wide to accept him. I want to...

"I want everything," I murmur.

He rolls me onto my back and in the next instant his mouth is on mine, not gentle, but not particularly harsh. Firm and demanding. Obviously taking control. The following seconds have my head swimming. His mouth is everywhere, as are his fingers, as if testing my limits. I wince only slightly when he unexpectedly twists my nipple between his finger and thumb, but then immediately follows the move with a swirl of his warm, soft tongue, eliciting a surge of desire that has me lifting my back off the bed, thrusting my breasts upward, demanding more of his attention.

While his mouth devours one nipple, a broad hand strokes down along my waist, along my hip, and grabs my ass. Squeezes. Hard, but not painful. An instant later, I feel the open-handed slap on my butt cheek. I giggle—

"Stop that!"

His firm tone of voice startles me, and I squelch the giggle as once again he squeezes my ass, harder than the first time, and then strokes his fingers along its contour, delving into that wet niche between my legs. He asserted his dominance with that tone of voice, and I realize... I realize that I like it, that sense of control.

My body is on fire. I want to roll onto my back, spread my legs, and reach for him, but he controls every move, giving me specific instructions to follow. Lie still. Don't touch me. His orders are clear. I want to touch him, to feel his strength beneath my fingertips. To wrap my hand around his engorged dick, but I can't. Not until he allows me to.

Instead of finding that off-putting, I find it titillating and exciting. After a few moments, I'm allowed to touch him where he instructs me to touch, stroke where he orders me to stroke. Squeeze where he demands me to squeeze. It's like nothing I've ever experienced before. Not quite gentle sex, but not dark and dirty either. He's a little rough, squeezing my breasts harder than I've ever felt before; he plucks my nipples, grabs a handful of hair and tugs my head downward so I can see his dick, but not to the point of causing me pain.

Rather, I find it invigorating. I feel empowered under his instructions, determined to follow through with his commands, to give him what he wants, and allow him to take what he wants from me.

Finally, every nerve in my body thrumming, afraid

that I'll explode, he seems to sense my need. Gasping for breath, feeling like I'm going to finish before he tells me I could, he flips me onto my back and spreads my legs. He half kneels between my legs, bending and pushing my knees apart. He stares at me, at my eyes, and then pointedly glances down at my breasts, his mouth slightly open, his pupils dilated. His gaze sweeps downward and fastens on my exposed pussy. My internal muscles contract under his gaze, and then his mouth is there, his tongue laving my lower lips, suckling on my nub, causing me to groan and lift my lips higher. I reach for his shoulders.

"Hold still. Don't touch me, " he orders, his voice vibrating against my mound.

It takes every ounce of my effort, but I place my hands at my sides, clutching the bedspread beneath me. His skin glistens with a sheen of sweat. I catch another glimpse of his engorged cock, but I can't reach it, can't touch it, as per his orders.

His lips and tongue work on my pussy, rough, but thrilling at the same time. He nibbles gently on my nub, and then I feel a finger plunge into my slit. I can't halt the moan that escapes my throat as I throw my head back, enjoying every sensation as that finger strokes in and out, his thumb circling my nub. I want to feel him plunging his cock deep inside me, but he doesn't. Not yet.

He shifts position, his lips and tongue still focusing on my wetness; he lifts his hands and grabs both my breasts, squeezing in a rhythmic action and then twisting my nipples and plucking at them with his index finger, repeating the process in time to his suckling. A myriad of different, slightly painful, sensations hum through my body and overcomes any sense of discomfort. The burgeoning flame in my pussy continues to rage, and then, his lips suckling deeply, his fingers twisting my nipples, I fall over the edge. Waves of contractions take over my body, take my breath away, and leave me laying limp and exhausted beneath him.

When I open my eyes, he kneels over me, his gaze riveted to my face once again. I glance down, see his cock, thick rope-like veins on its surface, thinking that now he'll take me, fully and completely. I can touch him. Finally, I can touch him.

Instead, he climbs off the bed and stands before me, allowing me to look my fill. But I want him back on the bed, next to me. I want to suck his—

"Next time I will take you, in any way that I wish. Do you understand?"

My arms at my sides, my knees still bent and spread, I nod, my gaze riveted on his face as he gazes down at me, his expression motionless. The only indication that he gained the least bit of pleasure from our... whatever this is, his dick, still jutting out at an angle from his body. He abruptly reaches for his clothes and then disappears into the living room. He's getting dressed. Is he just going to leave? Just like that? Without talking about—

He appears in the doorway, fully dressed. I look at

him, confused. Did I not please him? Is he disappointed—

"I'll get in touch with you after Christmas. We'll make plans."

Then he's gone.

8

DANIEL

I t's Christmas Day, but I'm having a difficult time enjoying the holiday. Ever since my rendezvous with Ashley at the hotel, I've had trouble focusing. As I turned from the doorway to the bedroom and left the suite, I had to fight the urge to go back and take her. Take her hard and fast. My body demanded it, but I quelled the urge. I'm the Master. I will not allow myself to be directed by my own desire for her, to feel this way.

Now, two days later, I still feel distracted. Growing up, Christmas used to be one of my favorite times of the year. When I was a child, my mother would go all out with the decorations, engaging her staff to hang Christmas lights, put up the Christmas tree, with boughs of Holly and garlands around the house and all that, but by the time I was eight-years-old, I realized that she wasn't doing that for me. She was doing it for show, for the parties she threw, the social event more likely an outlet for pent-up frustration and perhaps lingering grief rather than trying to make the holiday enjoyable for me.

I suppose it didn't really matter.

Even so, I did enjoy the holiday season in the city. The lights, the Yuletide spirit and everything that entails. I spent every Christmas with my mother, more out of an unspoken rule than preference. This year, I'm also spending the day with Karen. The two of them together. I sigh. They seem to enjoy each other's company, but I don't really want to spend time with either one of them. Actually, my presence at my mother's house today is out of my sense of obligation rather than any true desire to bond. As far as my mother is concerned, it's just another holiday, and that spoils the ambiance for me. Looking around at the decorations in the living room, it all seems rather pointless. Why does she still bother?

Since I arrived early this morning, Karen due to arrive soon, my mother has bedeviled me with questions about the upcoming marriage arrangements, the plans, the details, none of which I know nor care about. Karen is handling most of it. She doesn't ask my advice or opinion on anything, and I don't really want her to. I find it all rather tedious. I'm not looking forward to any of it. I don't allow my reasons for that to rise to the surface. Not today.

We sit in the living room now, she's sitting in her favorite white-upholstered armchair, so proper, so stiff, her cup of coffee balanced ever so carefully on the saucer resting on her knee.

I sit in the corner of the sofa, one leg crossed over the other, arms outstretched, my cup of coffee untouched on the table in front of me. Magazines fan just so, as if the housekeeper has taken a ruler to make sure that the arrangement of Home, Gracious Living, and Bon Appetit all appear equidistant to each side of the table.

"Did you hear me, Daniel?"

I glance up at her, an eyebrow lifted in question. "Sorry, what did you say?"

She frowns with disapproval. "I asked why you didn't attend the board meeting two nights ago? There are some important decisions to be made about expanding our reach into South America."

What can I say? That I was busy that afternoon indoctrinating Ashley into the world of bondage? That I originally planned to make the meeting, but because I'd taken more time with her than I had intended, at lunch and then in the room, I was running late? That I left that room in dire straits, considering that I didn't allow myself to achieve release, and I had to take matters into my own hand, literally, in the bathroom downstairs in the hotel lobby to seek said relief?

I almost smile. How would Mother respond if I actually admitted to such a thing? She'd probably have a heart attack. I sigh. "I talked to Roger yesterday. We're having lunch tomorrow to discuss those issues."

Her frown deepens. "Daniel, you know as well as I

do that the board meeting is the appropriate place to discuss such things. It's to be decided by everyone, not just you."

I shake my head. I don't want to argue with her today. "Actually, as the CEO, I have every right to make such decisions on my own." She begins to protest, but I lift a hand and stop her. "Don't worry, I'm not going to jump into anything without analyzing the data and consulting with the other board members. But I've been busy. I can't just drop—"

"You're running an international import-export company, Daniel. Your struggling publishing company is no match for—"

"We're not struggling," I say patiently, likely for the hundredth time since I've opened the business. "Actually, we're doing quite well. We have three releases this month, with excellent authors." I nod, thinking about it. "I've signed each of them to multi-book deals. Things are going well."

She says nothing but lifts her coffee cup to her lips, not glancing my way. I know what she's doing. It's that old mantra that I'd grown up with: if you can't say anything nice, don't say anything at all. Usually, she doesn't hesitate to speak her mind, but perhaps, like me, she doesn't want to spoil Christmas. As if.

I can't understand why my mother is incapable of supporting me in my true passions for what I want in my career, and life. True, my position as CEO of the family business is an obligation, but I take it seriously even though my heart is in publishing. She knows that, but she doesn't care, or at least act like it.

Which brings my thoughts—with a certain amount of resentment—to Karen as I glance at the clock on the mantle of the cold fireplace. She's late. Again. My mother calls her tardiness "fashionable" but I just find it annoying and rude. I sigh, shift my position on the couch, and glance around the room, neat as always; a place for everything and everything in its place. I grimace. What is with the Disney references? A Freudian desire to revert back to childhood, when things weren't so complicated?

Or on my sense of duty to my mother, whom I do love, which is the only reason I've allowed her to convince me that marrying Karen is a good thing? She doesn't know about my secret. She doesn't know about my membership in an underground and very secret society—

a club of sorts, where those with my... proclivities can indulge with others of a like mind without judgment.

I don't love Karen, I know that. I'm not even particularly attracted to her. She's beautiful, no doubt, but now that I've indulged with Ashley, I have trouble keeping my mind off her. I've never indoctrinated a newbie into the world of bondage, but her delectable willingness and enthusiasm during our first encounter, a pre-introduction into that world has gone so very well. My dick espouses interest at the memory—

I hear voices coming from the front of the house.

Moments later, Karen sweeps into the room, as she usually does, as if she's a movie star arriving on the red carpet. No doubt, she's beautiful, her corn silk waves draping delicately along her shoulders and her slender build by no means absent of voluptuous curves.

Still, as she arrives, much to the delight of my mother, I can't help but compare Karen to Ashley. Ashley being the opposite of Karen in hair color, height, as well as personality. When talking with Ashley, I feel myself attracted not only to her figure, but her large, warm brown eyes, quite different from Karen's dark blue eyes that rarely display any signs of emotion. She's cool, Karen is, and slightly haughty; a trait I normally admire in women, but that sense of aloofness carries over into just about every other aspect of her life.

I stand, as expected of me, forcing a smile toward Karen, who approaches with a smile on her lips as well, wraps her arms around me, and air-kisses each cheek. Still close enough to catch the hint of the aroma coming off her bright red lipstick and the floral perfume she wears, triggering an instant headache. I've politely—and repeatedly—asked her not to wear such fragrances, as they tend to trigger migraines, but as usual, Karen Queen does what she wants, when she wants, and however she wants.

"Karen!"

Mother greets her, animated for the first time since I arrived over three hours ago. I watch the two greet one another with true affection. They're birds of a feather, the only thing separating them in personality being their age. They're both pretentious, both drama queens, and not only competitive, but jealous in nature. At the moment, they were smiling, head-to-head, murmuring in French, which I never cared nor bothered to learn.

Finally, my mother turns to me with a smile, her hand clasping Karen's. "Karen just informed me that she's found the perfect florist to decorate the church for the wedding. Isn't that wonderful?"

I nod, pretending interest, wishing I were anywhere but here. I want to be back at my desk at the Pen and Quill. Familiar and comfortable territory. Even though it's Christmas Day, I'd rather spend my day editing than enduring... this.

I return to my place on the sofa and Karen follows, sitting close, reaching for my hand, leaning her head on my shoulder.

"You need to come with me to the florist the day after tomorrow," she informs me. "You have to help me decide whether we're going to go with roses or tulips."

I glance at her. "Tulips in winter?" I don't meant it to sound condescending, but as usual, Karen takes it that way. She lifts her head from my shoulder, pouting.

"Daniel, don't be that way," she says. "You know as well as I do that we're more than capable of acquiring tulips in wintertime."

She glances at my mother with a slight shake of her head. She fidgets for several moments, and then with a grin, which I suppose is meant to be seductive, she leans upward and whispers into my ear.

"Come with me upstairs, Daniel. I want to show you something."

I glance down at her, starting to shake my head. I'm not interested—

"Please, darling?" she purrs, casting a glance and a wink toward my mother. "It's important."

"Go ahead, Daniel," my mother says, sipping her coffee. "Indulge your fiancée... heaven knows you need to be more gracious with your time."

Before I can reply, Karen grasps my hand and tugs me out of the room and upstairs. She enters my old bedroom, shuts the door, and then pulls her blouse over her head, giggling softly.

"Come on, Daniel, won't this be fun? Fucking here in your old room while your mother sits below, waiting patiently for us to come back down? And on Christmas Day? Now, that's the kind of present I want."

So, I indulge her, without much effort or enthusiasm, but she writhes beneath me, moaning and groaning—

loudly at times—as if to prove to anyone in the household who just might be interested, that we're doing it in my old bedroom. As if anyone cares. I certainly don't.

9

ASHLEY

I spent an uneventful Christmas Eve day and Christmas Day dividing my time between my dad's house and my mom's, and of course, spent quite a bit of time over the holiday by myself in my apartment. My dad invited me over to spend some time at his place on Christmas Day in the afternoon, which was nice. I briefly saw my younger brother, Andrew, and his girlfriend, Melanie.

It was pleasant, but really nothing to rave over. My dad had put up one of those faux DIY Christmas trees in the corner with a string of lights, a few ornaments, and a few presents under the tree. I bought him a box of various tobaccos. An avid pipe smoker, he's somewhat of an aficionado, so I figured he would appreciate that. He bought me a sweater. I didn't get anything for Andrew or Melanie, nor did they get anything for me, which was just fine. Since he started dating Melanie,

Andrew and I don't talk as often. Understandable really, and I don't mind.

I usually keep so busy with work and fiddling with my writing that the days and weeks often speed by, so much so that weeks sometimes pass before I speak to any family members. But it isn't my manuscript or any work I am currently editing that has my thoughts occupied this Christmas. It's the memory of Daniel and I in the hotel room.

Every time I think of his gorgeous body, those gifted fingers, and his skill at provoking passion from my body leaves me rather stunned. I've never, never felt that way with a guy before. In fact, comparing my other experiences with that I've shared with Daniel, I realize that my sex life is incredibly bland and boring. And I wasn't even allowed to touch him!

Without admitting to myself that I'm actually desperate for Daniel's phone call or text message, or an email, as he promised, I try to bide my time. Still, every time I think about what he did to me; the feelings he evoked, the excitement I experienced, and the tingles of pleasure, I get hot and wet. So much so that while showering, I have to relieve myself, leaning into the corner of the shower, the water pounding down onto my breasts, my eyes closed and imagining that it's Daniel's fingers, his tongue, evoking those feelings and briefly releasing my passion.

After enduring two days where my thoughts are consumed with nothing but Daniel, and at times even forgetting that it's Christmas and my mind should be elsewhere, I start the day after Christmas with a resolution that I will take care of chores, maybe work on my manuscript a little, and practice patience.

Stewart left text messages several times, and called once on Christmas Eve, then once more on Christmas Day, hinting that we get together. I begged off, claiming that I wanted to spend some alone time with my family. He believed it, and while I felt a little guilty for lying to him, I saw no other polite way to avoid him. The thought of kissing Stewart now, or even sleeping with him left me feeling...

I'm not quite sure how to explain it, even to myself. He has the right equipment, but comparing him to Daniel... I shouldn't do that. Some people are just more experienced. It's obvious that Daniel is more than experienced in the sex department, but it's more than that. He's a Master. A Dom. And I desperately want to be his slave.

I try to distract myself yet again, gathering up a load of laundry and taking it downstairs to the laundry room. While waiting for the laundry to finish, I run the vacuum, do a little bit of dusting, and then open my refrigerator, thinking it's about time for a good clean out. I stare at the leftovers, the takeout containers, and the quart of milk already turning an odd tinge of yellow, and wrinkle my nose. I close the refrigerator door. Glancing at the clock, I see it's time to transfer the clothes to the dryer.

I head downstairs to do just that. Halfway down the stairwell, the phone in my pocket vibrates. I pull it out, my heart leaping with excitement, but dulling when I don't recognize the number. Not Daniel. I've been getting barraged by telemarketers lately, and at that instant, annoyed that Daniel is keeping me waiting, a relatively rare but ferocious streak of misguided revenge burgeons. While I usually ignore any call I don't recognize, I decide to answer this one. I'll remain silent, which often serves to annoy the hell out of the telemarketer after they go through their spiel.

I answer this call, ready to give the silent treatment, prepared for the instant rapid-fire promotion on the other end. I get nothing. Silence. I frown, glance down at the screen, and see that the call is still connected. Finally, a male voice speaks.

"Hello? Ashley?"

Oh my God, it's Daniel. I cringe. "Hi, Daniel," I say innocently, as if nothing happened. "How are you?"

There's a brief moment of hesitation before he speaks. "Can you meet me at the hotel today?"

I pause, halfway down the steps, my heart leaping with excitement, anticipation, and a surge of desire. "Sure, I'd love to. When?"

"Now."

I freeze. I took a shower this morning but didn't shave. Crap. I have laundry to deal with, and then changing clothes... all of which will take about an hour. I don't want to keep him waiting. Still...

"Have you changed your mind?"

I hear the change in his tone. Quiet. Firm. His "boss" voice.

"No, no I haven't," I say. "I just have to change real quick, but I can be there in about... twenty minutes?" I cringe again. What am I thinking?

"I'll meet you in the bar downstairs."

The call disconnects. I stare down at the screen, cursing myself, and then bolt down the stairs and into the laundry room. The wash cycle is complete, but I don't have time to wait for the clothes to dry. Yanking the damp clothes out of the washing machine, I smash them into the laundry basket, turn around, and race back upstairs. No help for that. I'll just have to wash them again later.

I quickly disrobe and rush into the bathroom, grabbing my can of raspberry-scented shaving cream from the edge of the bathtub. I quickly shave my legs, trim up my pussy hair, and quickly swipe the blade under my arms. I complete my ablutions in about three minutes. Dashing back into the bedroom, I open my closet door, nibbling on a fingernail as I try to decide what to wear. I finally groan, realizing it doesn't matter what I wear. Chances are I'm not going to be wearing those clothes very long anyway.

My breasts tingling with excitement, and my pussy offering throbs of anticipation, I quickly throw on a pair of jeans and a sweatshirt. No bra, no panties. Simple. This is me.

In less than ten minutes I'm out of the apartment, my heart pounding. Downstairs I push open the door of the lobby and step outside onto the sidewalk, wincing at the bitterly cold air that threatens to suck the air out of my chest. Thank goodness it isn't very busy. Being the day after Christmas with most businesses still closed for the holidays, I manage to hail a taxi in under a minute. I climb in, give the driver the address of the hotel and sit back, hands clasped in my lap to still my trembling.

By the time I enter the bar located on the west side of the hotel lobby of the Westin, I'm ready for just about anything. I think. I can't deny my nervous apprehension, coupled with expectation. It's kind of like opening a very special present on your birthday; not exactly sure what you're going to get but knowing that it's going to be good.

As I walk into the bar, I see Daniel sitting at the bar. It looks like he's nursing scotch. He isn't smiling. My heart skips a beat. Did I keep him waiting too long? Did he change his mind?

He turns and looks at me for several moments, gazing from my hair, which I pulled into a ponytail, to my sweatshirt, down to my jeans, and then my tennis shoes, sans socks. I stare back, waiting for him to laugh, to tell me to get lost, something, but after several moments, he merely grins. I allow myself a mental sigh of relief.

"You want a drink?"

He probably thinks I need to calm my nerves, but I don't need liquid courage. I need, want, to experience what he has to offer. I'm ready to open the door and experience the world that I've only read about. Do I need a drink for that?

"No thank you, I'm good."

He grins and downs the rest of his drink. "You ready?" He glances down at a small gym bag at the base of his stool.

I follow his gaze, briefly wondering what he has in there. In a matter of moments, I'll probably find out. In spite of my anxiety, I'm also more than turned on. This kind of attention, not to mention his charisma and his good looks, and the memory of his hard body, has my heart trip-hammering. I've only experienced a minute portion of his sexual prowess, I'm sure.

"Well?"

"I'm ready," I nod.

He abruptly places his glass on the bar, reaches into his shirt pocket and removed a twenty-dollar bill and places it on the bar. Without a word, he leaves the stool, reaches down to pick up the gym bag, and with his other, grasps my hand.

We walk out of the bar and into the lobby, heading for the bank of elevators. Once inside, the door dings shut and the car begins its upward journey. I imagine we're heading to the penthouse suite, where we enjoyed our previous liaison. What if—

"Today, we're going to focus on one of the scenes in your book. It has a few inaccuracies."

I glance up at him. "It does? Where?"

"The foundation of a beneficial relationship between a Dom and a sub is not just about control of the submissive," he begins.

His eyes lock on to mine, and I feel trapped there.

Not literally, but inside, I feel like I'm melting. Those eyes of his are so damn captivating, I want to stare at them all day.

"It's also about control of the Dom. Respect goes both ways in this kind of a relationship. It's not about fear, nor fear of punishment. Punishment should never be done in anger."

I think back to the multiple scenes riddling my book, but can't remember where I made such a mistake.

"Just remember, Ashley. Punishment doesn't equate to pain."

I don't know exactly what he's implying, nor the specific incident in my book to which he refers, but I'm grasping one concept. I want to learn. I want to learn from him. No matter what, I'm willing to try just about anything. I want to please him, not just sexually, but as his sub. As his partner, as his lover...

10

ASHLEY

As he takes me up to the hotel room, I can't stop my brain from going into overdrive. What if I discover I don't like it? Daniel promised that nothing would change, but it will. Everything will. How could it not?

If, after my first foray into this world, I decide I don't like it after all, what then? He will look at me differently. I will look at him differently. By the time I actually step into the hotel room, I'm close to freaking. Why am I flip-flopping all of a sudden? Why am I doubting myself? Why am I doubting Daniel?

And then he smiles at me. That's all it takes. A simple, encouraging smile. He points to a box. Not a large box, not one of those big, square moving boxes, but bigger than a box that stored file folders like you can get at your local office supply store. This box looks like the boxes we use to store a lot of the manuscripts that arrive at Pen & Quill that end up in the *maybe* slush pile. We hang onto them for awhile before either sending them back to the authors for more work or taking them down to the basement incinerator. And yes, the building is that old. It has an incinerator.

The box is set on the floor catty corner between the edge of the coffee table and the end of the sofa. What is inside that box? I know. It's a box of secrets, of sex. Can I deal with what's inside? I don't have any sexual hang-ups, but it's not like I often venture beyond the realm of what I call ordinary sex. Stewart isn't particularly imaginative nor have any of our sexual encounters gone beyond the norm. And by that, I mean, although not cruelly, the wham, bam, thank you ma'am, kind of sex. A few minutes of fore-play and then typically the traditional missionary position, and once or twice, oral, but still, very straightforward, very ordinary, almost... almost clinical in nature. I feel the heat of a flush warm my cheeks. What—

"Go ahead, open it," he says.

The box isn't taped, but the four flaps of its lid are folded in on themselves. One by one I pull the flaps open and then peer down into the box. My immediate impression? I don't see any handcuffs, and I realize that my conception and impression of bondage hovers on the naïve side. I cringe inwardly, realizing that in one of my scenes in my manuscript, I had the woman handcuffed to a bed frame with metal handcuffs.

Maybe that's what Daniel was talking about when he said he found some mistakes in my book.

I glance up at him, and he nods with encouragement. I begin to finger some of the items. I'm not surprised to find different gadgets of all sizes and textures. There are different types of rope, straps, and, much to my dismay, small link lengths of chain. I try to still my racing heart as I touch the items, but I don't remove them from the box.

"What are you thinking, Ashley?"

"I... I'm not sure," I admit. My fingers slide along the surface of a leather collar. It looks exactly like a dog collar.

"It's custom-made. Those metal rings are where rope can be secured or even attach a chain to it."

He speaks matter-of-factly. He speaks from experience. He *does* know this world. It isn't just talk. I don't want to look at him, don't want him to see my nervousness. Nevertheless, his voice compels me to.

"Most people use ropes, or rope-like devices, for their bondage encounters. That doesn't always mean a literal rope, like you had in another scene in your book. It can be anything such as a scarf, a belt, or even a necktie. Bondage is designed to restrict movement, actually. It's not meant nor intended to be a form of torture."

I don't have any torture scenes in my manuscript, so why would he say that? Then I remember. Another scene does have—

"It's not about rape, or even one-sided sex."

He sits down on the couch next to me, so close that his arm brushes against mine. I feel the heat of his body and inhale the scent of his cologne.

"Regardless of the tool of bondage, it's important to be very careful. It doesn't take much to cause rope burns or to cut off someone's circulation."

I glance at him, eyes wide. "I used rope in one of my scenes."

"Yes, you did," he nods. "And it was thick and rough. You described the kind of rope that they use in old Westerns to hang people or rope cattle with, didn't you?"

I feel like an idiot, but nod.

"If rope is used, it's most commonly a nautical type of rope made of nylon. Nautical rope. You know what I'm referring to? The white, soft, pliable ropes of different thicknesses?"

Again, I nod, absorbing his lesson.

"That type of rope is softer. When used in a bondage scene, nautical rope with a thicker diameter, not like the kind of rope you described, is preferred."

He pauses, looks down at the box, and then reaches into it. He extracts a two-foot length of white, nylon nautical rope, nearly an inch thick. He extends it toward me.

"Feel it. Run your fingers along the surface."

I swallow, but obey. I wrap my palm around the rope. It's sturdy, pliable, yet soft to the touch.

"Close your eyes. Imagine me tying you up with

this. You're bound to something with this kind of rope. What would it feel like?"

My pussy clenches as I imagine it.

"You can use this type of binding in any number of ways. You can tie someone's hands to the bedpost, like you did in your book, or you can be a little more creative."

I look at him. Creative? He stares back at me, a slight smile curving the corner of his lips. My nipples harden. Is he going to use this rope on me? Today? In a few minutes? As if reading my thoughts, he shakes his head.

"Rope is not used when a Dom and a sub are getting to know one another. The use of rope implies complete trust. Complete comfort with one another."

He takes the rope from my hands, his gaze not breaking mine.

"Always remember, Ashley, that allowing yourself to be bound is an act of complete submission. Whether with me or someone else, when you allow yourself to be bound, you're trusting the Dom."

He frowns and tosses the rope back into the box. "What is it?" Did I say something, imply something with a look? He looks at me, and for a moment I don't think he's going to answer.

"I knew a couple, not that long ago. She was accidentally killed by her Dom—"

I can't help the gasp that escapes my throat. I stare in dismay.

"They had been drinking. Oh, what they did for

their scene wasn't unusual. He bound her wrists and then, using another rope, bound her to a large hook screwed into the ceiling."

I imagine that, a woman, naked, arms raised over her head, totally at the mercy of her partner. "What happened?"

"They indulged, but because he was drunk, he more than likely missed the cues that she gave him." He looks out the window. "Remember the safeword I told you about?"

I nod.

"No one really knows for sure what happened. Even the guy couldn't completely recall the course of events. Anyway, the autopsy determined that she had been bound too long. She was inebriated, too. Rule number one: You don't do scenes when you're drunk."

He looks at me again, pointedly, and I nod. I feel like a bobble head.

"Her position decreased oxygen intake, and she had difficulty breathing. She didn't use her safeword, and if she did, she didn't say it loud enough or he wasn't listening. The strain on her lungs also placed a strain on her heart. She died."

How awful! How could something like that happen? Why didn't the guy follow the rules—

"They'd been married for ten years. They had two kids. CPS took the kids, and he's in jail for manslaughter."

I swallow a hardened lump in my throat. How horrible—

"I'm telling you this because the rules have to be followed. If they're not, bad things can happen." He sighs. "Most of the people in this world that I know are businessmen and women; they have careers, families, and children. You wouldn't know what they do behind closed doors just by looking at them."

I understand what he's trying to say. I watch him for several moments, contemplating his somber expression. He isn't looking at me anymore, but into his memories. I pull my gaze away from him, allowing him this moment of... of grieving? I glance back at the box. Okay, so ropes are out for now, especially ropes suspended from ceilings.

I see a metal contraption. It looks like a bar, maybe a foot long and an inch round. Holes are drilled into each end of the bar. An S hook feeds through those holes and connects to a couple of large leather cuffs, padded on the inside with sheepskin-like material.

"What's that?" He glances down to what I point out and smiles as he lifts the bar from the box. Watching me. As if to gauge my reaction.

"This is a spreader bar. They're usually two or three feet long, although of course, size and construction varies. It's intended to separate extremities." His grin broadens. "For example, I could place the cuffs around your wrists, or around your ankles, keeping your legs spread. Easy access."

The heat of a flush travels all the way from my chest upward into my face. *Stop that!* I imagine myself lying on the bed in the other room, naked, my ankles cuffed, the bar spreading my legs while he—

"Want to give some of this a try?"

An equal surge of heat builds in my groin, causing internal contractions and a surge of wetness. After only a few seconds of thought, I nod. This is what I want, isn't it? An adventure? A teacher?

"But not here," he says.

I'm confused. Why did he bring me up here again? Were we going to have another round of what I consider vanilla sex? He sees my consternation and chuckles.

"We can't use most of that stuff in here. I brought you up here, Ashley, so that you could look at some of the tools used in bondage without being overwhelmed or..."

"Chickening out?" I glance down at the gadgets in the box. He chuckles once more, sending a jolt of anticipation through my body.

"If you're ready, we'll go to a home I own, not far from here. It's private and secluded."

I lift an eyebrow. "You have a house, here in the city, in addition to your penthouse apartment?" I grimace. I just committed a faux pas. I'm not supposed to know that my boss has a penthouse apartment, am I? Any more than he should care where I live.

He merely grins. "Yes, in addition to my penthouse apartment, and equipped with a basement that I've converted into what I call my playground."

He studies every nuance of my expression. I get it.

He can't be seen taking women into his penthouse apartment, risk anybody hearing them—

"Your playground," I murmur. What other gadgets does he have in this playground of his? I can only imagine—no, not imagine. Experience. He's inviting me to his playroom.

I don't know if he's daring me or expecting me to back out or what, but I accept his challenge.

"Lead the way," I say, hoping that my voice expresses more bravado that I feel at that moment. I can't back out now. I want to learn. I want to know everything there is to know about this world that Daniel seems to enjoy so much.

11

DANIEL

She's game. I have to give her that. Despite the content of her manuscript, which only skims the surface of the bondage world and is riddled with a number of errors that only a true Dom or sub would recognize, I also know that she has zero experience with the real thing. Not really. But reading about something and doing it are two different things. Night and day. The look on her face when she gazed down into my little box of tricks was unmistakable. She might've seen pictures of some of that stuff online, but there's no way she has ever seen any of it for real.

She doesn't strike me as the kind of person who would go to an adult store and buy things like this. I seriously doubt it if she's ever ordered anything online. No, she's too innocent. Not naïve, but innocent. There's a big difference. I like that about her. She's eager. She wants to know. She wants to learn. Whether she's truly curious and wants to get involved in my world or she's doing this to become a better writer, I'm not sure. It doesn't really matter. And who better to teach her? I'm not thinking that in a bad way. I'm not taking advantage. She's been given plenty of opportunities to back out, and I will continue to give her those outs. I won't force her into this. She has to choose.

I look forward to being her mentor and her teacher. At the same time, way in the back of my mind, I'm a bit concerned about how this will change our relationship; not just our professional one, but privately.

I'm to be her Dom, she my sub. Before we get started, I will reiterate the rules. Not just the rules of the games, but my relationship rules. Our *playtime* will be nothing more than that. I have no expectations of her beyond my playroom, nor will she have any expectations of me. The characters in her manuscript are more than Dom and sub. They're partners. They're lovers in the truest sense of the word. I don't need that. I don't want it. I already have my hands full as it is.

We're in my gray Porsche 911 Carrera S Cabriolet, driving toward the house I own in a quiet little neighborhood on Long Island. Ashley is quiet, admiring the interior of my car, glancing out the passenger side window, looking everywhere but at me. I get that. She has lots to think about. I see the pulse throbbing in her neck. She's nervous. Understandable.

The house on Long Island is my secret place, my literal hideaway. No one other than the few subs I take there on a regular basis know about the place, and I've sworn them to silence. They have no doubt that I would come down hard, really hard, if they betrayed my secret. I don't have to threaten or intimidate. The people involved in my secret world also want to keep their secret. Those not in this world wouldn't be apt to understand that you can wear a business suit during the day and a leather hood at night...

My mother doesn't know about it. Karen doesn't know about it. The deed is in the name of one of my holding companies used for shipping to and from Manilla. Buried deep in my business affairs. I want to keep it that way. This home on Long Island is my haven, my sanctuary, the place where I can be myself.

Sure, I indulge with Crystal in my office on occasion, and a few others a time or two; one of the reasons I had the entire space sound-proofed one weekend, paying extra for the workmen to work around the clock to get it done.

Once in a while, I indulge in hotel rooms, to an extent. But my playroom? That is one of my favorite places. I designed it carefully, ordered particular pieces one at a time. Of course, I don't have the accoutrements of my hobby shipped directly to my house, that wouldn't do. That holding company I hide deep in my business life also owns a warehouse down by the docks. Stuff I order arrives there and then I either hire a rental truck myself, or I pay someone to bring the stuff over, after making sure, of course, that no labels or markings on the box in any way hint at its contents. No sense broadcasting my bedroom proclivities to the community where I purchased the two-story brick home, with a basement of course, dating back to the 1920s.

On the outside, my home is classy, the yard and landscaping always well-groomed thanks to wonderful gardeners; the house set back a short distance from the street, bordered by a tall hedge. It's perfect.

By the time I pull into the driveway, I feel my dick coming to life. At the same time, I'm more than aware that I have to ease Ashley into my world. No way can I fuck her the way I fucked Crystal on top of my desk in my office. I don't want to.

I don't want to fuck Ashley. The term seems too crass for her, but I don't want to make love to her either. Our playtime isn't about romance. But first, I have to wait and see how she reacts to my playroom. If she seems at all hesitant, I told myself that I won't be disappointed, that I will casually offer to drive her back to the hotel, the office, or to her apartment, whichever she chooses, without a word. But oh, do I want her to stay. I want more of her; more of what I've gotten from her in a hotel room, sensing that she needs to drop that oh-so-proper veneer of hers; that she will bloom under my tutelage.

Shutting the engine off, I turn to look at her.

I can tell by the look on her face, those wide eyes taking in everything, that she's trying not to look astonished or impressed. Still, I watch her gaze sweep over the landscaping, the brick façade of the house. She wants to take in everything from the front steps to the top of the dormer windows on the second floor.

Is she more surprised to think that this sedate, innocent looking twenties-era house has a basement filled with bondage play toys or is she impressed by my wealth?

It doesn't matter. I'm not here to impress her, and she isn't here to get all googly-eyed over my property. I decide to nip that in the bud.

"Why are you doing this, Ashley?"

She turns to me, eyes widened with surprise. "Because you said you had a basement—"

"No, that's not what I mean." I turn to gaze at the house and then back at her. She appears confused. "Before we get started, you need to know a few things about me. One, I'm private. This house is private. No one at work is to know about this house. Do you understand?"

She nods.

"What goes on here is not to be discussed with anyone, not even your BFF, Tory, nor your boyfriend, Stewart, nor written about in any personal papers, such as a diary. Understood?"

She nods again and opens her mouth as if to speak, but I hold up my hand. "Let me finish." She nods. "Finally, you should know that you're not the first, and you're not going to be the last woman that I bring here to play with. I'm telling you now that I don't want any indications of jealousy on your part. Understood?"

I know I'm being a little harsh, but these things need to be said. Clarification is important. I made that mistake once, several years ago, and I'm not about to make it again. No strings. No attachments. No obligations.

"I understand," she says quietly. "And I'm doing this for two reasons. One is professional, the other more personal."

"Explain."

"You said that some scenes in my book are wrong, or least not accurate and detailed enough. I want to improve that. I want to hone my skills as a writer. If I'm going to write in that niche, I have to know what I'm talking about."

I nod and gesture for her to continue.

"The other reason, the personal reason, is because I feel... well, I've felt that there's been something missing from my... sexual growth. I can't think of any other way to put it. With Stewart, things are rather..."

"Boring?" She has no idea. Sex with Karen is so typical, so bland, so... routine. Nothing special, nothing passionate, nothing to get overly excited about. Perhaps that's why I indulge myself as frequently as possible in this world. I need some kind of excitement to make me feel alive. To make me feel... like Ashley, I'm not quite sure how to put it. It isn't just about sex. It's so much more than that.

"Yes, boring." She glances out the window at the house. "And don't worry, I'm not looking for any attachments." She looks back at me. "I've got enough going on in my life right now without anyone making more expectations on me. I'm here to learn, Daniel. To experience. To explore this world and see whether it's something I can embrace."

"You're not sure?"

She frowns slightly. "Of course, I'm not sure. I've never done this before. How can I be sure of something I've never tried?"

I hold back my smile. I'm glad that she has the confidence to respond honestly. "Okay then. From the moment we go downstairs to the basement, you are my sub. You will do as I say, when I tell you to, and how I tell you to do it. Understood?"

She nods. Satisfied, I turn and open my door, looking forward to the next couple of hours in my playroom.

"In order to gradually introduce you into this world, you have to learn about the authority of the Dom. The Master. Me. In your book, you have a scene where your characters are literally playing on equal ground. In many scenes, it's not that way." She opens her mouth and I hold up my hand. "You will only speak when I give you permission to speak."

She frowns. She will learn, given time. "As you can see, I have a number of tools and objects in here."

She gazes around my basement, carefully decorated and painted to convey an aura of a dark underground shelter. A different world from the brightness and traditional ambience upstairs.

She eyes the table in the middle of the room with a combination of curiosity and wariness. She stares at the two 4x4 posts bolted onto the floor about four feet apart and the bank of mirrors in front of it, taking up much of the long wall. A few hooks and gadgets hang from the ceiling, but we aren't going to go there this afternoon. Not yet. Hooks on the other two walls hold a number of other tools and toys ranging from leather whips to a number of belts, a couple of the spreader bars as I showed her in the hotel room, and even a couple of riding crops. I have paddles of all shapes and sizes. Her eyes widen noticeably when she looks at the hoods, the face masks, and ball gags also hanging from hooks on the wall.

I imagine what she's thinking when she eyes the gags. I want to soothe her worries, but the moment we entered the basement, I became the Dom and she my sub. "When a gag is used, I'll give you something that you hold onto. See those rubber balls and those small jingle-like bells over there?" I point to a small table in the corner, draped by a black cloth, fitting in to the dark décor of the room. The table holds an assortment of bells and balls of all shapes and sizes, some solid, some not. She nods.

"If a gag is used, I typically offer my sub a ball or a bell. You hold onto that. If a safeword can't be used, dropping the ball or ringing the bell will signal that you're having some type of problem and trigger a time out."

She nods, appearing relieved. I frown. "Those are

not to be used lightly. You wanted to be introduced into this world. There is some pain involved, but I don't dole out pain without also rewarding with pleasure. The safeword and the safe tools are *only* to be used if you experience some trouble like difficulty breathing, or you can't deal with the pain."

She remains silent, eyeing all the items in the room with curiosity. I continue to speak, purposely keeping my tone soft but firm. There will be times when I'll be rougher, firmer, and more in control, but scaring her off at this point will serve neither of our purposes.

"Whether you're with me or someone else, you need to always be aware of what is acceptable and what is not. A Dom should never strike you in the face." I extend my hand, palm up. "I *will* deliver soft to moderate open-handed slaps on other parts of your body, but never your face."

She nods, looking up at me, her features calm though the pulse thudding faster now in her throat belies her expression.

"I will never break your skin deliberately. Sometimes, you will experience some chafing, maybe a scratch or some bruising depending on the tools we use, but we'll take care of those after the session or the punishment. Do you understand?"

Again, she nods.

"One more thing. I will never leave you alone if you are bound in any way. Before you indulge in any kind of this activity with anybody else, you better trust them. You better trust them not to do that to you. Is that understood?"

Another nod.

"I know we covered some of these things before, but I want you to understand, and I mean seriously understand, that while the entire purpose of this is bondage and my dominance over you, it's not torture. It's not supposed to be about torture." She looks up at me. "Speak."

"I understand, Daniel."

"I'm not sure you do, at least not yet," I murmur. "Like I said, I noticed a number of errors in your book in regard to types of punishment and domination that you described. Let's just say we'll look at each one and experience each one in turn."

I can tell she wants to ask something. "Speak."

"How many types of punishment are there?"

"This world is more than physical domination. Of course, you're aware that bondage implies restriction. Some Dom's use humiliation on the sub." Her eyebrows lift in question. I hold in my grin. She wants to ask questions. Lots of questions. I decide to indulge her curiosity without giving her another chance to speak. If she can't handle that, she won't be able to handle many other things I consider doing to her. With her.

"I know some Doms subject their subs to several types of humiliation. Some make them eat from a dog dish on the floor. I've known others who urinated or defecated on the sub." She blinks, but other than that I don't see any reaction. "Personally, I find that type of punishment repugnant, and I've never treated my subs to that type of humiliation. But to each his own."

She nods, and I continue. "I am a physical and verbal Dom. In this room, you will always refer to me as Master." Again, she nods. So very eager to please. "I can use any of these tools to portray my physical dominance over you," I say, gesturing to the various tools and gadgets in the room. I take on a firmer tone. "You will do what I say or you will be punished. Understood?"

At first, I think she's going to smile, but then she changes her mind. Smart. "This isn't a joke. Now's your chance to change your mind. If you're in this, you're in it one-hundred percent. If you're not, I'll take you home right now."

She says nothing. "Speak."

"No... Master, I'm in it, one-hundred percent," she says.

"Good. Then let's get started."

My heart skips a beat. Here we are. Time to pay up or shut up. Sure, I'm a little nervous. Who wouldn't be the first time they're introduced to an actual bondage scene? I'm not sure what to expect. Daniel has been good about explaining some of the ground rules, but talking and doing are two different things.

"So what's it going to be?"

I look up at him, at first confused. What is he asking me? Which toy I want to play with? I wait for him to give me permission to answer.

"You will answer me when I ask a question."

But he told me not to speak until— "I... I'm not sure—"

"The safeword has to be something that has nothing to do with sex or anything involving any of these activities," he says, gesturing around the room.

A safeword. He's talking about the safeword. I think about it a moment and then reply, "Apples." He lifts an eyebrow.

"Apples?"

I nod. "I like them, it's a short word, and I don't see any apples in here."

He almost grins. Almost. Then he heaves a heavy sigh and frowns. I'm nervous, no doubt about it. I've never been a submissive before. With Stewart, I typically let him do what he wanted, but it was all very basic, very quick, and he never felt inclined to try something new, different, or anything close to what was hinted at inside this room with Daniel.

How will I react to being spanked? How will I react to having my nipples twisted? It isn't just—

"Get undressed, over there in the corner. Fold your clothes and place them on the chair."

I swallow, look over into the corner, and nod. Making my way over there, I can't stop my heart from trip-hammering with anticipation and yes, I'll admit it, a bit of uncertainty, maybe even a smidgen of fear. I know that Daniel won't hurt me, not in the cruel sense of the word. I have my safeword, and if I don't like what he is doing I can use it and he will stop, right? What if I don't want to do something that he does? What if I have to do something I don't like, and he demands it?

At this very moment, I realize that submission isn't going to be easy, at least on my part. It isn't necessarily about what *I* want to do. At the same time, I also realize that I can't just throw out the safeword any time I'm hesitant or because I don't want to do something. The safeword is about safety, not about preferences.

I hear him moving around in the room, but I don't turn to look and see what he's doing. I was told to remove my clothes and fold them neatly, and I did, one at a time. I decide that I will only use the safeword if I feel that my very safety is at risk or if it will cost me some type of physical damage. Daniel already told me that he doesn't approve of some behaviors, and I have to trust him on that. I also sense that he won't be apt to ask me to do something that would be horrible.

Completely disrobed, I stand in the corner facing the wall. I feel a little funny, standing here naked, displaying my ass to the room, but I'm not sure what to do now. Should I turn around and approach, or should I wait for him to tell me to do so? I have a lot to learn. Boy, do I have a lot to learn.

"Come over here."

I turn around and barely refrain from gasping when I see him standing there, next to the upright posts, stripped out of his previous clothes and now wearing what looks like a pair of jogging pants, although quite loose and flowy.

"I said now!"

I startle and tug my glance from his pants up to his face. He isn't smiling. So much for starting out on the right foot.

"Come over here," he says, pointing to the floor

between the two posts. Resisting the urge to cover my breasts, I walk toward the posts. What does he think of me, walking toward him, buck-ass naked? Are my breasts large enough? My areolas too dark? Did I shaved my pussy hair acceptably? I never go totally bare down there. After all, I don't want to look like a five-year-old. Stewart wanted me to shave completely, but I felt it was kind of pervy of him to even ask me to do that. I believe I'm groomed neatly enough, shaved short and narrow, but that's as far as I go.

I notice him staring down at the apex of my thighs. He didn't say anything the first time we had sex in a hotel room. If he asked... no, told me to...shave, would I?

He says nothing as he turns me toward the mirror and then takes one of my hands. He reaches for a leather cuff with sheepskin padding affixed to a foot-long and medium-sized chain. Though I can't imagine what he intends, I watch silently as he buckles the cuff to my wrist and then hooks the chain with a heavy karabiner to an eye-bolt screwed into one of the posts just over head height. He repeats the process with my left hand, and then each of my ankles.

He steps toward a light switch on the wall by the stairs and turns off the lights to the room. Only one light stays on; a recessed, flush-to-ceiling dim light that shines down on the two upright posts and my naked, splayed body, as if I'm standing center stage. I am.

To say that I feel vulnerable is an understatement.

He strolls around me, staring at every part of my exposed body. I try to watch him, but the moment I turn my head, he swats my ass and orders me to look at the mirror and not move. I obey. He stops behind me, able to look over the top of my head, staring at my reflection in the mirror.

I barely squelch a yelp of surprise when his fingers grab my ass cheeks and squeeze. Hard, but not hard enough to bring tears. Immediately, all my muscles clench. I have to force myself to relax. Heart pounding, I feel his fingers sliding between my legs, exploring my slit. This time I gasp and shift slightly.

With one hand between my legs, the other grabs a handful of my hair and pulls until my chin lifts toward the ceiling. His voice is thick, and the whisper of his voice wafts against my ear.

"Don't move or you *will* be punished."

I think the anticipation of what he is going to do, where his hand will roam, is the foundation of an increasing sense of anxiety. Not scared anxiety, but uncertain anxiety. In the next few moments, my uncertainty fades as he stands behind me, his chest pressed against my back. I feel his large, hard erection against my ass crack. He shoves his hips forward, and I brace my feet and resist, trying not to move, as he instructed.

I kept staring at the mirror, not daring to look around though every cell in my body wanted to turn, wanted to wrap my arms around him. That isn't what this is. For a brief second, I feel a surge of disappointment. Will I never be able to hold him? Caress his fine, hard body? Never—

He releases my hair. Both of his hands sweep around my waist and cup my breasts, his thumbs swirling around my nipples. I bite back a moan as an almost electrical stimulus jolts my body, starting behind my breasts and shooting all the way down to my groin. My pleasure disappears when both thumbs and index fingers squeeze my nipples. So sensitive, never experiencing anything like that, I utter another gasp as unexpected and unwanted tears fill my eyes. The startling jolt of pain fades as he immediately swirls the pads of his thumb over my nipples, replacing the pain with soothing pleasure. And then he does it again. Pain, not unbearable, followed by pleasure. After the first time, I'm not so surprised. I realize that while the tweaking and twisting hurts, the expectation of pleasure soon to follow has me actually looking forward to it.

He pauses a moment, and I feel him moving behind me. What is he doing? I feel slick wetness between my legs and my pussy clenches with anticipation. His chest presses against my back again, the heat of his body close to mine. His engorged cock nestles against my ass. No fabric separating us now. He's warm, huge, and solid.

His cock thrusts between my legs. I stare at it in the mirror as it peaks between my legs. He squeezes my ass once again and then his hands grope my breasts.

Pinch, tweak, pull, against my nipples and then his thumbs swirl around them. He begins to move his hips, his cock appearing and disappearing at the apex of my thighs, sliding against my slit, making me wet, hot, and ready. My hands clench, my jaw tight as I struggle not to make a sound, not to move an inch.

Goose bumps rise on my flesh when his tongue licks at the back of my neck, sending shivers of delight racing down my spine. I absorb every sensation. Not even the hard smacks against my ass can take away the hot pleasure of his tongue trailing down my spine. His body shifts, his cock disappears, but with his left hand still squeezing and plucking at my nipple, his other hand alternately slaps and squeezes my ass cheek. Every once in a while, he moves that hand and strokes it between my legs, eliciting another surge of hot liquid. My pussy contracts. I can't halt the moan that erupts from my chest.

He grabs at my hair and pulls my head back, hard, my jaw once again facing the ceiling. Tears glisten in my eyes. The brief surge of pain disappears when his teeth nibble on my ear, following the next instant by his hot breath against that very same ear.

"If you move again or make a sound, I'll gag you and punish you."

Shame on me, but I want to know what that's like. I speak without permission. "Daniel, please—"

"You are to call me Master!"

I can't help but stare at my wide-eyed reflection in

the mirror—my eyes shining, my mouth open with desire, my body splayed. I want to see what he's doing but it's dark beyond that tiny circle of light. He walks away from me and surprisingly, I feel bereft. My body grows chilled. His warmth and attention drawn away from me, I can only stare into the mirror, trying to discern his shadow in the darkness of the room behind me.

I can't see him. What is he doing? Did he leave? Am I to be punished with his absence? He told me that it was against his rules to leave a sub bound, but where did he go? My pleasure subsides as my worry intensifies. "Daniel? I mean, Master? Where are—"

I hear the crack of sound before I feel it. The sting of leather on the flesh of my ass. I can't deny it. It hurt! But before the sting of the slap dissipates, I feel his cock in between my thighs again, pumping faster.

"Watch."

His tone is on the back of my neck again, one hand grabbing a fistful of my hair, forcing my eyes back to the mirror. I watch as his cock slides back and forth between my thighs. When is—

He bends me forward, pressing down on my neck, my arms stretched to their limits. I bite back a gasp as the sudden, rough move startles me. Immediately after, I feel his cock probing my wet slit. My pussy responds.

"Beg for it!"

His voice is the same. This is Daniel, my boss, but hearing him talk like this, in that deeper voice, that rough, guttural voice with an edge to it, I know this is a part of him that he keeps well hidden from ordinary people. I'm excited and a bit awed at the same time.

"Beg for it! Beg for my cock to dive in!"

"Please, Master," I respond dutifully, meaning it. "Dive in!"

Once again his cock disappears, as do both his hands from my body. His lips find my shoulder, that spot between the base of my neck and the top of my shoulder, and he nibbles. He uses his teeth, scraping them along my flesh. I know he'll be careful not to leave marks, at least not obvious ones. More goose bumps. I pant with anticipation. I hear him tear something open and recognize the sound. A condom. Thank goodness one of us is thinking. I didn't even give it a thought. Not just about protecting myself from an unwanted pregnancy, but an STD. Maybe that's something we should've talked about before, but—

Both his hands grab my shoulders press me down and forward. Once again, my shoulders ache at the stretching. My head immediately drops downward, but he grabs my hair again, forcing my head up.

"Watch!"

I do, embarrassed and fascinated at the same time. I've never watched myself having sex before. I've never watched— His head probes between my legs for several moments, and then pauses.

"Beg for it!"

His voice is gravelly, strained, as if he's holding himself back. "Take me, Master!" I gasp. "Please!"

He obliges. With one, single, hard thrust, he enters

me. Fills me completely, almost painfully. It feels like I'm not big enough for him, that I can't hold him, but once he's inside, he pauses, giving me time to adjust. Not nearly long enough. I want to relish this moment, but he's the one in control.

His hips begin to thrust. His dick slides nearly all the way out and then surges upward again. Hard. Forceful. I wince, but try not to make a sound. I hear the slick, wet sounds of him entering and withdrawing. Hear the sound of his balls slapping against my ass and upper thighs. I want to touch him, to grab that huge cock, but I'm bound and unable to move. I'm not sure if I'll be able to—I have to distract myself or I'll finish before he does. I force my eyes to watch his face. So fierce now, so handsome. Both of his hands grip my shoulders, hard, both of us staring into the mirror, watching as he pumps into me. My knees want to sag, but his grip tightens. I keep my eyes riveted to his face, see his jaw clench, then his chin lifts slightly as he rocks his hips, slows down his pace only slightly, and then, in three more pumps, he climaxes.

I'm not sure if I can let go now, if I can—

His cock still captures inside me, he moves his hands off my shoulders, wraps them around my waist and once again cups my breasts. This time his fingers massage, twirl, and gently pluck and twist. One hand continues to tweak my breasts while his other roams straight down my belly until he cups my mound. I watch him fingering my nub and that's all it takes. Punishment and pleasure. Pleasure and punishment—

two more strokes and I feel waves washing over me. Blinding, breathtaking, white flashes of waves. Waves of pleasure wash through me, around me, and have my head swimming.

I've never, ever experienced anything like this. I want more. So much more.

13

DANIEL

In the past few hours, I introduced Ashley to several of the gadgets in my playroom, and after using the devices on her, explained several naïve mistakes she made in her manuscript regarding a number of scenes in her book. I have to admit that I'm impressed. She's an eager and willing student. I can't even begin to count how many women I have fucked over the years, but there's something different about Ashley. It isn't just the fact that I, an expert, am introducing her to this new world.

It's that we seem to connect on a level I didn't expect. Her body seemed to sense what I needed before I did. She enticed me in ways others haven't, and she wasn't doing it on purpose. She's a natural. Her passion is unmistakable. No, her breasts aren't extraordinarily large; rather they are a large B cup, maybe venturing into C territory. But more than a handful is a waste anyway, right?

I don't think my reaction to our playtime had anything to do with the fact that I had never done this with her, either. I never *tutored* anyone before. I had many encounters with women I had never met before, nor after. But there is something about Ashley that just seems so fresh, so... I can't even name it.

She dresses slowly. I watch. Now the shyness has returned. Not overt, but I sense it. Perhaps even a touch embarrassed, but she's game. I like that about her. That mixture of naivete with such a zest for adventure. Coy shyness that's natural, not faked. Her pleasure wasn't faked either. I know that she gained pleasure from our exercises. I also gained pleasure. It was a win-win.

I went so far as to contemplate inviting her to the bondage club. I've never even considered bringing someone to the club. I never really felt like I needed to. I get everything I want there and then some. Plenty of women and couples looking for partners. For different kinds of sex. No questions. No demands, no strings.

This thing with Ashley, this feeling she gives me... I feel relaxed. It's more than just getting my rocks off. I actually enjoy spending time with her. Today wasn't so much about release as it was in exploration, seeing this world through fresh eyes. Usually after a scene, I'm ready to go. I hate lingering. I despise women who want to linger with me afterward. Crystal learned early on that our interactions were about one thing and one thing only. Fast, hard, hot sex. She wanted to be dominated and I wanted to dominate. With Ashley, it's a bit different.

Yes, I'm still her Dom and she my sub, but there's a sweetness about her, something that I can't quite wrap my mind around.

I realize I'm lingering. Taking pleasure in just watching her get dressed. I watch every move, every tilt of her head, the way her hair drapes over her face as she bends slightly to don her pants. I watch her fingers as they slip on her tennis shoes. I smile. This is a new feeling, and I like it. I don't want it to be over.

Thoughts of work, of my mother, of Karen, of the demands everyone place on me are gone. I'm just living in the moment and enjoying every second of it. Ashley stands and turns to me. She isn't sure if she can approach or whether she should stay until I tell her she can move.

"I'm just Daniel now, Ashley," I say. "Come over here."

She does, smiling hesitantly, glancing at me and then quickly glancing away. Her cheeks are still flushed, her eyes glistening. "So, what do you think?"

She opens her mouth to speak, then closes it, slightly shaking her head before trying again.

"I— I was surprised by a few things, and I was more than startled a couple of times, but I liked it."

She's honest too. This world is still new to her. No amount of research can compare to the real thing. "You think you learned a few things along the way?"

"Yes, I did. And you're right. If I'm going to write about it, I have to know what it all feels like. The thoughts that goes through your mind when..." she pauses. "I'm blabbering," she admits, offering a slight shrug.

I know her well enough now to know that the slight shrug is a sign of awkward embarrassment. "No, you're not blabbering. I want you to benefit from these... lessons," I say. "It will make your writing better."

She dips her eyes and nods, not looking me in the eye. What is that? Disappointment? I'm not going to tell her that this has been one of the most invigorating afternoons I've spent in a long time. I'm not going to tell her that I enjoyed myself supremely, that she was a most willing pupil, and a good one at that. I can't go there. She has to know that this—our sexual encounters—are just that. Sex.

Is that the only reason I brought her down here to my playroom? It was part of it, yes, but after reading her manuscript, I couldn't deny my curiosity. Only part of my curiosity was assuaged this afternoon. There is so much more to learn about Ashley— I stop myself right there, straighten, and gesture toward the stairs. "We should go."

No. I absolutely cannot get involved emotionally with Ashley. As I watch her walk across the basement floor toward the stairs, I realize with surprise that keeping my distance will be a challenge. Especially after what we just did. She made it possible for me to feel completely relaxed and at peace. I can't remember the last time that I felt this way.

While it would be interesting to take her to the

club, I also decide that she isn't even close to being ready for such an adventure. One step at a time. We walk upstairs and at the landing I gesture down the short hallway toward the kitchen. "There's a bathroom just off the kitchen if you need to... use it or clean up or anything."

She smiles and nods. "Thank you, I'll just be a moment."

She walks off down the hallway, her tennis shoes barely making any noise on the wood floor. No sharp clack of heels that usually grated on my nerves as I waited for my subs to leave. I follow her several moments later and enter the kitchen area, where I open the refrigerator and pull out two cans of diet soda. I pop one open and chug down half of it before she emerges, her hair slightly damp, her face fresh. Holding my half empty can of soda, I gesture toward the other one.

"Thirsty?"

She smiles and reaches for it. "Thanks," she says, popping the lid.

If she's surprised I offered her a soda and not a drink, she doesn't acknowledge it. She takes several sips and glances around, trying not to be overt about it.

"Would you like a tour?"

Her eyes widen but she nods. She takes a sip and then places the can back on the counter.

"You can bring it with you," I say. Sipping from my own can, I give her the grand tour. Another first for me. Not one of my subs, not one, have ever been allowed past the kitchen door and into the rest of the house. In fact, the kitchen bathroom is as far as any of my previous "guests" have roamed in this house. I've never offered any of them anything, not even a glass of water. The basement playroom is one thing, but the rest of this house is my private domain. One I keep to myself. This place is only for me. Not Karen. Not Crystal. Not anyone. But I find myself wanting to share it with Ashley.

I shove thoughts of Karen out of my head. Playing the gracious host as I give Ashley a tour, listening to her murmurs of appreciation in regard to the structure, the décor, and the overall ambience. She laughs softly as we return to the kitchen.

"What?" I ask, honestly wanting to know. Another first.

"I think I can fit my entire apartment into your living room," she comments. "You have a lovely home here, Daniel."

I can tell she wants to ask. Why I keep the house a secret. She's a smart girl. I'm sure she can figure that one out on her own.

She takes a last sip of her soda and then places the nearly empty can back down on the counter. She's had enough. I reach for it, tip the can upside down into the sink, and listen to the remainder trickle downward. I follow suit with my own, then toss both cans in the trashcan under the sink.

"Let's go."

We make our way back outside to my car. "You

want me to drop you back at the hotel or the office, or do you want me to take you home?"

She hesitates only a second. "Can you take me back to the hotel? I have a few errands I need to run in the neighborhood anyway."

I nod, somewhat relieved that she didn't taken me up on my offer to take her to her apartment. I feel torn. Torn between wanting to get to know her on a deeper level and wanting to keep her at arm's length. No entanglements. No promises. No strings.

14

ASHLEY

It's New Year's Eve. I haven't heard from Daniel in a couple of days, and I'm not sure if I'm disappointed or whether I'm expecting too much. My introduction into genuine bondage down in his basement playroom in his secret house left me tingling for an entire day. He dropped me off at the hotel like I asked, but I didn't really have any errands to run. I just didn't want him taking me to my apartment. I didn't want him to see where I lived. Didn't want him to realize that I wasn't his type after all.

I wasn't embarrassed, as I like my apartment, but compared to that house of his? It's like comparing peanut butter to caviar. Face it. I'm a simple girl. Not typically impressed by wealth or material things, I felt myself rendered somewhat speechless while Daniel gave me a tour of his home. Well, not really his home, because I do believe he spends most of the time in his penthouse apartment downtown.

Still, I've crushed on the man for such a long time. Being given a glimpse into his world, aboveground and then to his basement playroom, gave me a deeper glimpse into this person that I've admired secretly and from afar for so long. I admire and respect him as a publisher, but until a couple of days ago, I didn't even imagine the various facets of who Daniel Stone really, truly is.

I like him even more for it. Dammit, I can't allow myself to get any more emotionally involved with him than I already am, and that's entirely one-sided as it is. I have to know where to draw the line between the fantasy I developed within the pages of my manuscript to the reality of life.

"Did you hear me, Ashley?"

I'm jolted from my reverie, the steady beat of the party music once again pounding inside my brain. I'm at Tory's, at her annual New Year's Eve party. It's crowded, almost claustrophobic in her packed apartment. Does she really know all these people? It seems like it. While I'm not much for partying, I need a distraction. Usually, I spend New Year's Eve alone, preferring to watch the shows on TV, and sometimes even to go to bed before the ball drops. This year, no. I need to be surrounded by people, by the music, the dancing, and yes, even some harmless flirting.

I know I'm allowing myself to get too wrapped up in Daniel. The past couple of days, I've barely gone ten minutes without thinking of him. I can't do that. Not only is it not part of our "deal", but I can't allow myself to go falling in love with him. It would be so incredibly easy. I've admired him for so long, secretly created this fantasy life with him, that after the basement, those feelings burgeoned even deeper. Without even trying, he hooked me. I want to continue exploring his world, to spend time with him, but I can't get clingy. If I do, I don't doubt for a moment that he'll cut me loose.

"Ashley!"

"What?" I finally reply.

"Here comes Stewart!" Tory says, pointing.

I see Stewart enter the apartment, doing his impersonation of John Travolta in Grease. It used to be funny, but now it's just embarrassing. He looks like he's already had a few. His gaze sweeping the crowded room, he finally sees me, lifts a hand, and begins pushing his way through the crowd in my direction.

I smile politely as he approaches, wraps his arms around me, and plants a wet kiss on my lips. His breath smells of beer and whiskey. I responds only slightly, thinking that at some point, I have to break this thing off with him. It isn't going anywhere. Not where I want to go, anyway. I know he wants a more serious relationship, but the thought of spending a life with Stewart is just... sad.

At some point, I need to make it clear to him that not only am I not interested in marriage, but we aren't in an exclusive relationship either. He has no idea how I feel about Daniel, and I'm not about to tell him.

It's impossible not to compare the two now. Different as night and day, not only in the sex department, but in persona. Stewart is a nice guy. He really is. There's only one way I can think to put it. Stewart is vanilla, and I want Rocky Road. Stewart is plain and boring; at least that's how I feel at this point in my life. I want texture, adventure, and never knowing when I'll bite into a marshmallow or a nut, or just enjoy the silky smoothness and flavor of smooth chocolate.

I sigh. I don't want to hurt Stewart, but I also feel that stringing him along isn't fair to him nor myself. But not right now. I can't tell him tonight. The countdown has started. Less than two minutes until midnight. At the minute mark, Tory turns off the music.

"Watch the clock, everyone!"

Everyone in the room turns and begins to count down. I join in, feigning exuberant joy over a new year, Stewart beside me. One arm draped over my shoulder, his other hand reaches for mine. He squeezes, but I don't squeeze back.

Thirty seconds until the new year. A new year. New adventures. New hopes and dreams. A fresh start. Letting go of the baggage, I can think of a million ways to express how I feel at this moment, but all I can do is watch the second hand count down on the clock. I feel Stewart's eyes on me, but I refuse to look at him, pretending that I'm enraptured by that second hand, slowly clicking down to the ten-second mark.

The room bursts with excitement as everyone begins to count down the last ten seconds of the old year, preparing to ring in the new. At the stroke of midnight, everyone cheers, laughs, and claps. Stewart turns me toward him and wraps me in his arms, kissing me. I kiss him back, but my heart just isn't in it.

"Come home with me," he says, practically having to shout to be heard over the revelry. "Let's ring in the new year together!"

I shake my head and decline. "I'm sorry, Stewart, but not tonight." I should tell him the truth, but I can't, not right now. Instead, I lie. "I promised my dad I'd drop by."

"I'll go with you—"

"Thanks, Stewart, but no. I'm just going to stay for a minute, and then I'm going to go home and crash. I'm exhausted."

I see his disappointment, but I stick to my guns. I have to start breaking away, and the longer I draw this out, the worse it will be for both of us.

15

DANIEL

I sit at the kitchen table across from my mom, asking myself for the tenth time since I arrived what the hell I'm doing here. All I can think of is Ashley and the fun we had down in my playroom. I can't get her out of my mind, and I can't figure out why. Yes, she's different and yes she's fresh, and I do enjoy being her teacher, her Dom, but it's more than that. This relationship between us is turning out to be more than just sex and that's what confuses the hell out of me.

I've never had this happen to me before. I've never got to the point where I felt personally connected to my subs. Is it because I knew Ashley from work before we developed this relationship, or is it because of her? Ashley. No pretenses with her. No fake persona. No trying to impress me because of who I am. No, Ashley is just Ashley. I've watched her interactions with others in the most innocuous of places; smiling to someone crossing the street in front of the car, the genuine kindness and skill with which she counsels our authors, the way she speaks to clients or peers in person or on the phone. She's nice. She doesn't look down her nose at those less fortunate.

"Are you listening to me, dear?"

I glance at my mom, watching me with an odd expression, her head slightly tilted to the side. "I'm sorry, my mind wandered."

"Your mind has been wondering quite a bit frequently," she says, frowning. "Are you concerned that your wedding date is fast approaching?"

Karen. I'd been to a New Year's Eve party with her the night before. I'm not much for New Year's Eve partying, more preferring to stay at home. It isn't that I mind the social interactions, but to me, people make a way bigger deal over the new year than I think necessary. It's just another holiday, right? All this crap about new beginnings, new dreams, new resolutions. Most of them recycle from the year before. It's foolishness. It's a day just like any other, just marked differently on a calendar.

"No, Mother, I'm not."

"Then what is it? What has you so distracted? Is there something going on at your publishing house?"

"No, everything is fine there, actually. Everything is perfect." That isn't a lie. All is good in the world of Pen & Quill. And with one of my new favorite employees. I almost smile.

"Then what's going on? What's the matter with

you? You seem so distant lately. More distant than usual."

I smile then. I can imagine what she would say if she knew what really has me distracted lately. And I know where she's heading with her line of inquiry. Karen wanted me to spend the night with her last night after the party; wanted to ring in the New Year with a romp in bed, but I couldn't do it. I demurred, blaming it on having had too much to drink, coupled with a headache and an upset stomach. Of course, that was the wrong thing to say because then she'd wanted to nurse me back to health.

Karen is beautiful. She's a catch by any man's standards. But I can't help comparing her to Ashley. I've told myself to stop it, that doing so is pointless, but there it is.

"Daniel, talk to me. What's gotten over you this past week? You're just not acting like yourself."

Acting like myself. For the first time in a long time, I feel like I can act like myself, at least with Ashley. No pressure. No pretending. When I'm with Ashley, I'm not a billionaire. I'm not the CEO of a huge company, nor even the owner and managing editor of a publishing company. I'm her Dom. We're sex partners. I'm her mentor, introducing her into a world that I have a feeling she's wondered about for quite a while. Her manuscript is proof.

We've enjoyed two visits to my basement playroom since that first time. She's a natural. She didn't try to overplay her role, as some other subs did. She didn't exaggerate. She didn't act like she was an actress performing for the camera. Her little gasps of surprise delighted me, so much more than the fake screams and desperate pleading of Crystal or another one of my subs. She obeyed but at the same time, and for the first time, I also wanted to make sure that she gained just as much pleasure from the experience as I did. Another first.

"Daniel, you're doing it again!"

I look at mother, staring at me, her fingers lightly clasping her silver-plated fork, poised over spinach quiche. I notice the untouched glass of orange juice in front of her; the tablecloth white and spotless, her posture perfect, her earrings and bracelets matching the highlights in her gray cashmere sweater with its oriental style and gold-embossed collar and cuffs. Everything about her perfect. No hair out of place. Makeup exquisitely applied. She doesn't go around like one of those older women with powdered faces that don't match the color tone of their neck. No, not my mother. She always makes sure that she's presentable. Perfect.

Though Karen takes great care in her appearance, and spends hours on it, she doesn't have quite the same sense of style that my mother has. She works too hard at it. And Ashley? I barely hold back a smile. She's a jeans and T-shirt kind of girl, which is actually quite refreshing. And she doesn't care, which makes her confidence even more appealing.

"Daniel, you tell me right now what's going on," she orders.

A spot of color appears on her cheeks beneath the pinker shade of her blush. She lowers her voice and inhales, calming herself. Order restored.

"You had better not spoil this, Daniel. You need to put your priorities in order. Don't forget you have responsibilities—"

"I know that," I say. "Nothing is sliding. I'm on top of things."

"Then I ask again, what has gotten into you? Why on earth have you grown so distant these past few days? Not only with Karen, but with me?"

She places her fork on the plate and folds her hands underneath her chin, her perfectly manicured fire engine red fingernails rounded just so, contrasting with her pale skin. Here it comes.

"Karen told me that you two were at a New Year's Eve party last night and you refused to take her home. That doesn't sound like you. Did you two have an argument? I know how stubborn you can be, especially—"

"Mother," I say as patiently as I can, "Karen and I didn't get into an argument."

"Then why didn't you—"

"Mother, I'm not going to discuss my sex life with you."

"She's worried about you, honey. You know that you can always talk to me, right?"

I nod. Sure I can, if I want every word I say to get back to Karen, which I don't. For the moment, I merely need to mollify her concerns. "I had too much to drink last night. I just wanted to go home and go to bed, all right? It doesn't mean that anything is wrong."

I haven't touched my food. I reach for my fork, hoping to end the conversation. It don't work.

"Don't mess this up, Daniel. Karen's a wonderful match for you. You know that, don't you?"

I say nothing. I can't deny that my mother is quite fond of Karen. At first, that was somewhat of a relief. Now I'm not so sure. Most of the time I feel like it's two against one. I know that at some point I need to put my foot down, but sometimes it's just easier to go with the flow.

"You need to focus on your responsibilities. That's all I'm trying to tell you."

I stab my quiche. "Mother, I'm thirty-five-years-old. Karen will turn twenty-five this year." I sigh, as if worried. Mainly to see if she'll back me up or Karen. "Sometimes it just seems that my head is in a different place than hers. That's all. I've got a lot on my plate, and I didn't feel like partying. I had too much to drink, and all I wanted to do was go home. By myself. If Karen wanted to stay out and party, I wasn't going to stop her."

Her response is expected; still, it lets me down.

"I realize the age difference can cause some problems, dear," she says, lifting her fork again. "But do what you can to keep her happy, will you? She's adorable, and I like her very much. Yes, she has some growing up to do, but with her social status, her upbringing, and her family connections, this is a good thing."

I've lost my appetite before I've taken one bite and place my fork back on the plate. "Mother, I understand how business connections work. Family ties and all that. But to be brutally honest, Karen cares more about the materialistic things than—"

"You have to be patient," she interrupts. "Yes, she's younger than you, but she'll mature. You just have to give her time."

Time. Time will not change Karen. Time will only make her worse; more condescending, more demanding, more annoying. Ashley is only a couple of years older than Karen, but she has her shit together. She has a job that requires not only skill, but the ability to work under pressure, under deadlines. She just doesn't edit for the sake of making sure that all the Ts are crossed and the Is dotted. Ashley works hard with every author to make their books the best they can be. She cares. She's invested.

Come to think of it, I've never even asked Karen what she wants to do with her life. What does she want two years, five years, or ten years down the line? Where does she want to be? She comes from prestigious ancestry, from old family money. Unfortunately, I quickly learned, from my mother no less, that her family money had just about been depleted, which is why Karen's parents' approached my mother. To make a deal, throwing the family back into the seventeenth century with what my mother called a "merger marriage". I called it something different. A marriage without emotion or affection and disregard of faults. With this marriage, Karen's family will get the money they need, and my mother and the family company will get the political connections that my mother feels we need to move up.

That's what Karen wants. To move up. But move up to where? I have no political aspirations—but maybe she and my mother feel that's where the 'up' is. As far as I know, my mother hasn't dabbled in politics. Ever. So what is the ultimate goal? It has to be the money. Karen probably bleeds green for all I know. I shake my head. I have to remember that I don't have to love Karen. I can still have my secrets. My subs.

I didn't refuse my mother's request for me to marry Karen. Why? I still can't understand it. Is it some pseudo-psychological need in me to finally do something that pleases her, that will convince me that she loves me, or—

I grunt and turn to look out the window. What the hell? I didn't really care all that much about the entire deal until now. And why is that? Because I read Ashley's manuscript. Saw in her... what? A kindred soul? What a sack full of shit. Still, there it is. The two women are as different as night and day.

When I met Karen for the first time, she had regaled me ad nauseum about the years she attended boarding school in France, her world travels, and her family's ancestry. Supposedly they came over on the Mayflower. Trying to impress me. She tried too hard, and I saw right through it. She was all shiny on the surface and more than easy on the eyes, but I had yet to find any real substance underneath. Sometimes when we went to a function or a dinner, she even spoke with a French accent to fool people, or so she said. To me it came across like she was just trying to lord it over them. Yes, Karen is beautiful, but she is a drama queen; she can be quite pretentious; and to make matters worse, she's a manipulator. She pouts to get her way with me. With others, she orders, and if she doesn't get what she wants, she makes their lives hell.

When we met, I hinted that I'd had sexual relationships with women in the past. That was to be expected, she'd said, automatically assuming that since we'd met, my dabbling days were over. She merely shrugged and intimated that such was to be expected of men, but after we were married, my dabbling would of course cease immediately. About a week after that, she backtracked slightly and, in not so many words, intimated that she didn't care if I dabbled once in a while, as long as it was kept secret and I didn't develop any kind of a serious relationship with the woman in question.

Once the agreement of our match was settled by our respective parents, she came right out and told me that it didn't really matter to her what I did. But I had already begun to believe that she viewed me as a possession. One to hold but not to cherish. As far as she was concerned, appearances were essential. I know she doesn't love me, any more than I feel anything for her. What I do get from her is that I'm "hers". Basically, if she can't have me, no one else will either.

What the hell did I agreed to? And how in the hell can I tell that to my mother? If I back out now, she'll be humiliated, a subject of gossip, and believe me, I know how fast and ugly gossip travels in this town.

Karen puts on such a good front when we're around our respective parents. Actually, Karen's parents as well as my mom honestly believe that Karen is head over heels in love with me. She isn't being cruel to my mother. She actually likes my mother a great deal. She said they are two birds of a feather. I believe it.

So, there is the question again. Why did I allow myself to be talked into this? At first, I didn't think it really mattered. My mother would get the political clout she seemed to think we needed—that our company needed—along with another network of potential partners, clients, and associates. She can't possibly think she's actually doing me a favor... finding me a wife, a partner? I sigh. If she only knew...

"You'll think about it, won't you, Daniel?"

I glance up, not even bothering to ask what she was talking about. I totally spaced out. I nod, offering a small smile. "Of course, I will." That seems to calm her, whatever was talking about, and we both finish break-fast; she with a self-satisfied smile, and me just going through the motions with only one thought in my head.

When will I see Ashley again?

16

ASHLEY

I'm back at work, trying desperately to concentrate on my job. I think I've read the same manuscript page five times but my mind keeps wandering. The holidays are over. Time to get back to work. After taking several days off over the holiday season, I'm woefully behind.

Unfortunately, I'm so distracted it seems impossible to focus on editing. I read the words on the computer screen, dotted with red font that substitutes for my red editor's pen, but all I can see in my mind's eye is Daniel. Great. It was bad enough when I had a one-sided crush on him, admiring him from afar. Now? Did I just drop into a rabbit hole? Am I destined to make my life miserable because of my growing attraction to him? Even at that moment, trying to concentrate, I know what is happening.

The newness of our secret relationship is not solely to blame. For me, spending time with Daniel is exquisite. It isn't just the sex either, which, after a few experiments, I found far less intimidating and much more invigorating than I ever imagined. That basement of his...

"Stop it," I whisper, once again forcing my attention back to the manuscript. I can't allow myself to grow attached to Daniel. Impossible. I'm good at keeping my feelings to myself, or at least I am unless I put them down on paper. As in my manuscript, where all my inner feelings have been allowed to see the light of day. On my laptop. If I hadn't left my laptop open, if he hadn't read my manuscript, if we hadn't "indulged" in his basement playroom several times already, I wouldn't be in this position.

I'm not sure which was worse. Admiring him in secret or growing fonder of him with every moment we spend together. Even though I know that my attachment to him won't be reciprocated, at least not in the way I would like, it's still better. Being with him is better. He's fascinating. Handsome with a gorgeous, hard body. But oh, so much more than that. I want to know everything there is to know about Daniel Stone. Not his resume. The person. At the same time, I know doing so is fruitless.

Daniel made no promises. Nothing of the sort. I know that he isn't just mentoring me so that I can write better. I also know I'm not his only sex partner. It's obvious by his experience and confidence in that underground world that he belongs to, and apparently has, for quite some time. And along with that world comes a multitude of sexual partners and subs. I understand that. At the same time...

"Ashley!"

I glance up at Tory's hiss, her eyes wide and one hand, hidden from view by others in the room in front of her chest. Her index finger pointing down the hallway, at the end of which is Daniel's office. My eyes widen when I see him standing near the end of the hallway opening into our large office space divided into cubicles, frowning.

"Didn't you hear him? He's asked for you twice!"

I shake my head to clear my mind, nod in his direction as I stand, ignoring the curious gazes from not only Tory, but two other editors as I cross the main room and approach Daniel, straightening my skirt as I go. Rather proud of my performance, I smile as I approach.

"I'm sorry, Mister Stone, I was embroiled in a manuscript-"

"If you have a moment, I'd like to talk to you about the Jespersen manuscript you edited last week."

"Of course," I say, following him down the short hallway to his office. His expression appears harsh. Am I in trouble? Did he change his mind about us? My mind jumps from one worry to another. Is he going to curtail our secret relationship, or even worse, fire me? I shake my head. Don't be stupid. Nothing is wrong. Our interactions at the office have to continue as they always have. Pure business. I'm quite proud of the work I'd done on the Jespersen manuscript. I can only wait and see what he wants.

I follow him into the office. He shuts the door, locks it, and then practically body-blocks me from entering the room. My back bumps against the door and he raises both hands and places them on either side of my shoulders, effectively trapping me. I stare up into his green eyes, uncertain. Why is—

"Take your clothes off," he growls.

I stare up at him, startled as a flush of heat rises in my chest and travels up my neck until my cheeks flame with heat as well. "Here?" I gasp. "You want me to take my—"

One hand moves quickly, grabbing a handful of my hair. He takes a step closer, his gaze never leaving mine. My scalp tingles. His other hand leaves the door and gropes my breast. I immediately feel a surge of wetness between my legs and my nipples tingle. He wants to—

"I said to take your clothes off. If you don't obey, you're going to pay for your lack of obedience."

My heart skips a beat. He's serious. He wants to... in his office, in the middle of the day! I know I have to obey, but at the same time, what if somebody—

His grip on my hair tightens. I wince. Without further thought, I quickly unbutton my blouse. He watches my every move. My trembling fingers unlatch my bra, which hooks in the front. His gaze dips from my face down to my breasts, and I feel my nipples harden under his gaze. I waste no time unzipping my skirt, stepping out of my slip-on flats, and divesting myself of my thong. I stand naked in front of him, waiting for his next command.

"Blow me."

Again, it takes my mind a few seconds to catch up with his words. As I stand there, dismayed, his hand moves. A second after that I feel the open palm of his hand slap the side of my ass. I gasp.

"Did you hear me? I said blow me."

Praying that no one will knock on the door, that no one in the outer office had any indication of what we are doing in here, I quickly nod and reach for his belt.

"No."

His grip on my hair forces my chin upward, forcing me to look up at his face. His expression blank, his gaze roams my body. I glance quickly away. He stands so close that I feel the bulge in his trousers.

"Faster."

I glance up again to find him looking at my face, no clue as to what he's thinking, but my fingers work faster. He doesn't want me to unbuckle his belt, so I proceed to lower his zipper. He remains silent. I reach inside and feel thin fabric. Boxers. I find the opening and reach for his cock. It's rock hard. I wrap my hand around it and maneuver it upward along his inner thigh until it juts from his pants. I glance down at it, not sure exactly—

Both hands on my shoulders, he pushes me downward. Kneeling. His engorged penis aims straight at my face. His hands leave my shoulders and grab either side of my head.

My heart pounding, I take him into my mouth. For several seconds, he remains perfectly still. I freak a little bit, because I don't particularly like doing this, not with Stewart, not with any of my previous boyfriends, and maybe not—

"Suck harder."

I tighten my lips around his head. I grasp his cock at its base with one hand using a firm grip, slowly stroking and laving his shaft with my tongue while at the same time minimizing the length his dick can reach into my mouth. I have a pretty good gag reflex, and if—

"Let go."

His dick still in my mouth, my hand still wrapped around it, I glance upward. He isn't looking at me, but staring at the door, jaw tight and eyes half-closed. I don't want to let go. I don't want him shoving his cock down my throat. I don't want... should I use my safe-word? No. He isn't hurting me, he isn't putting me in any danger, but I definitely don't want... it isn't about what I want. At the moment, it's all about what he wants. Reluctantly, I release my grip on his cock. I continue to suckle, my hands braced against the outside of his rock-hard thighs. He presses his hips forward, his shaft sliding deeper into my mouth. His head touches the back part of the roof of my mouth. Instinctively, I pull my head back. He growls low in his throat and tightened his grip on my head.

"Don't move."

I still myself and continue to suck, gradually increasing pressure, then easing back, all the while his hips begin to thrust a bit harder, a bit faster. And then it happens. His dick goes too far. He holds my head in a vice-like grip and I panic. The gag reflex kicks in and I barely prevent myself from biting him while a horrid sound rips from my throat. My grip on his legs tightens.

He freezes. I squeeze my eyes tightly shut, not wanting to look up at him. I don't want to see anger or annoyance. I feel embarrassed, but I can't help it. So, I kneel there, his cock in my mouth, my tongue hesitantly rolling over his head. He says nothing but he lets go of my head.

Wanting to please him and make up for the fact that I gagged... actually gagged... I continue the momentum while he stands perfectly still. I worship his thick, pulsating cock with my tongue, suckling for a second, then using my tongue to stroke along his length. I pause to suckle again on his head gently, even once or twice nibbling softly at the tender, glistening flesh there. I make a humming sound deep in my throat, but they come out more like passionate moans, which they actually are.

My own desire surges. My breasts ache for his touch, as does my pussy, gently contracting and relaxing in much the same rhythm as my mouth along his cock. I continue to moan, not because he asked me to, but because at this moment, I'm supremely happy and self-satisfied with myself. I can't believe I'm doing this; giving Daniel Stone a blowjob in his office while just outside the door my peers work away, none the wiser. He shifts and his hands clasp my shoulders.

"Get up."

I release him from my mouth and immediately stand, looking up at him. His pupils dilate, he stares down at me and then gestures with his chin toward his desk.

"Go stand beside my desk, facing it."

I do as he demands, but not before I glance down at his engorged shaft. It's dark, throbbing, pulsing with a life of its own, the veins threading along its surface filled with pulsating blood that causes that shaft to do a little dance of its own. His head glistens with moisture. I walk over to the desk and stand with my back toward him. He approaches from behind.

"Bend over and grab each corner of the desk with your hands."

I face the narrow side of his desk and do as he asked, my body tilting slightly forward.

"Back up," he commands.

His hands on my hips, he forces my feet to move several inches back.

"Spread your legs."

I do and hear him move toward the window. I hear a zipper and then a rustling sound. He kneels and grasps my left ankle and wraps something soft around it. I hear a clinking noise, and then realize what he's doing. A leg spreader. It's maybe twenty-four inches long. In a matter of seconds, the cuffs are placed around my ankles. I lean over the desk at a forty-five-degree angle. He adjusts my positioning to exactly how he wants me. Occasionally I feel his cock brush against my thigh or my ass. My wet and throbbing pussy aches for him but he takes his time. The anticipation is killing me. I want to tell him to hurry, but I can't. He's the Master. Not me.

I hear him shuffling nearby, then the sound of tearing. The snap of plastic. Another surge of wetness moistens my slit as I realize he's slipped on a condom.

"This room is soundproofed," he says. "But I don't want you to make a sound. Do you understand?"

I nod, swallowing. He had his office soundproofed? When? How— What is he going to do? Why would I scream—

In one, swift, powerful thrust, he enters me from behind, surging deep into my wetness. It's so hard, so fast, and so unexpected that I can't prevent the gasp that escapes my throat.

"I told you to be quiet!" he hisses.

A hand reaches under my arm and grabs my breast, squeezing. I wince but keep quiet. Several seconds later his grip eases and his fingers tweak my nipples. Touch gently and then grope again. Pain, pleasure. Pleasure, pain. Not blinding hot pain, just enough to awaken my nerves. His hips thrust forward forcefully. Even through the fabric of his trousers during that brief contact, I feel his heat, the occasional brush of his legs against the back of mine. Despite my awkward positioning, I feel my own desire burgeoning. Every time his cock fills me and he dives deep inside, I feel as if I'll burst.

He remains perfectly silent, only his hips moving. His breathing grows harsher and deeper. He pushes down against my upper back, so much so that my face is nearly pressed onto the surface of the desk. I desperately want to let go of that desk, to reach back, to touch him, anywhere, but I don't dare. And then, with two final thrusts, I hear the soft, rumbling groan rumble upward from his chest.

Finally, he stills. I don't move, my own body humming with electrical, stimulating sensations. Still buried deep inside me, he wraps his left arm around my chest and lifts me upward while his right hand reaches around my hip and gropes my mound. Held captive in his embrace, my back pressed tightly against his chest, his thumb and fingers work at my slit until my hips begin to rock of their own accord. He stops fiddling with my nub and grabs my right hand, encases it in his, and then lowers it once again to my pussy. Together, my hand encased in his, he brings me to the fullness of my pleasure. I climax, my body held firmly against his, his dick still deep inside me. I barely manage to prevent the moan of pleasure that escapes, although I do throw my head back against his chest. I feel his harsh breath against my ear as the waves of ecstasy sweeps over me, so much so that my knees nearly buckle. I don't have to worry. He holds me up.

Panting, my body feeling boneless, I sag against

him. My ears ring and my head stops spinning and gradually clears. My eyes focus on the clutter of paperwork on his desk. He kneels behind me and unbuckles the leg spreader. I don't move.

He points over my shoulder toward the small bathroom door. "Go get yourself cleaned up."

17

DANIEL

I watch Ashley walk toward my office door, where she stoops down to pick up her clothing before stepping into my private bathroom. Her back to me, I admire her shapely figure. I love the way her narrow waist flairs slightly into gorgeous, well-shaped hips. Her ass is firm and tight. I could probably stick a quarter between her ass and the top of her thigh and it would stay there. Athletic, although I don't think she's engaged in any sports. Maybe she had an active childhood. I don't know. Maybe—

I don't allow my mind to wander, but force it back to the present. I feel satiated. I feel more relaxed than I have in a long time. Even my interludes with Crystal often left me feeling dissatisfied, or actually un-satiated; as if something was never quite finished, not sexually, but emotionally, or maybe even mentally.

I shake my head as I reach for the box of Kleenex in my top desk drawer and remove the condom, bundling it up inside the Kleenex, and then another, before wadding it all up and throwing it in the trash can. I tuck myself back in my pants, zip up, and adjust. I hear the water trickling in the sink in the bathroom.

I glance up at the clock on the wall. She's been in my office less than ten minutes. No one will wonder about that. Still, I don't want her to linger. Not because I don't want to spend more time with her, because God knows, I do. But not here. Not in my office.

Maybe later tonight, or tomorrow—

My cell phone rings. I move to my desk and reach for my iPhone and turn it over. The light blue background of the screen distracts me from the bathroom door, behind which Ashley is probably— I glance down at the screen, scowling when I see the caller ID.

Karen. My sense of relaxation, that elusive sense of calm that enveloped me during those few blissful moments with Ashley are doused as effectively as a bucket of cold water thrown over my head. Poof. Gone. Immediate tension, annoyance, and dissatisfaction surge upward. I sigh and answer the call.

"Hello, Karen." What will she complain about today? Probably that I didn't show up for the cake tasting appointment yesterday or maybe because I didn't make a final decision on the floral arrangements? I don't have time for this. I told her—

"Hi, Daniel. What are you doing?"

For a second, I consider telling her the truth. "I'm working."

"What are you working on?"

What the hell? For a brief second I think she might be suspicious, that her bat radar has picked up on something in my voice. Or perhaps she has a hidden camera in my office or something. I shake my head, feeling stupid. "A manuscript," I answer. "What do you need? I'm busy."

She makes some pouting sounds, then chuckles softly. Before Ashley, and in the early days of our faux relationship, that throaty chuckle was enticing. Sexually charged. Now it just grates on my nerves.

She gets to the point. "Fine. I know that you gave me charge over all the decisions regarding the wedding, but honestly, Daniel, I don't feel comfortable doing all of this by myself. You are going to be part of this marriage, after all. Do you think you could work up some enthusiasm and take on a couple of the tasks yourself?"

"I don't know anything about planning for a wedding," I say, my gaze flicking toward the bathroom door as it opens and Ashley steps out. She's all put together again, although her cheeks are still flushed. I gesture for her to sit in the chair in front of my desk. At least for a minute or two until some of that color leaves her cheeks. She might as well be wearing a flashing sign that says 'I just got fucked by my boss'. I grin at her. Her cheeks blossom with color.

"It's not like you have to plan anything, Daniel. But do you think you can squeeze enough time into your day to make some calls to a couple of country clubs in the next day or two? I've got the church taken care of, but I'm not sure where I want to have the reception. I'm overloaded with the florist, the baker, the wedding planner, choosing the décor—"

I sigh. "All right, I'll try to make a couple of calls. But seriously, can't you ask my mother to help? She knows more about this stuff than I do."

"She's already busy with the caterer, the menu, and working on place settings."

I tamp down my annoyance, wondering for the hundredth time why I allowed myself to agree to this. "All right, I'll take care of it. I have to go now."

"I'll see you later this evening. We're having dinner with your mother, remember?"

"I remember, Karen. Goodbye."

I disconnect the call and toss the phone onto my desk blotter. Ashley look at me. "My fiancée," I explain. "Wedding planning stuff."

"You're engaged?"

I nod. She shifts in her chair, her back straighter and her expression blank. She has to know sooner or later, if she doesn't already. I don't go around talking about Karen or anybody else in my social circle, but I know how gossip moves through the grapevine, and in the publishing house.

"Congratulations," she says. "When's the big day?"

"Thank you," I say softly, sitting behind my desk. "And it's coming up."

She doesn't say anything more but glances down at her fingers, crossed in her lap. The color has eased out of her cheeks. I glance around my desk, grab a printed reader's proof for a manuscript sitting on the corner, and hand it to her.

She takes it, her brows slightly furrowed.

"I called you into my office to go over a manuscript. It will look a little odd if you don't leave my office with said manuscript, don't you think?"

With a nod, she takes the manuscript, then looks at me. I can tell by her questioning gaze that she isn't sure if we're still in that Dom/sub roll. We aren't.

"Are you all right?" I ask, indicating that our roles are over.

"I am," she says, glancing down at the manuscript. "Well, I guess I'd better get back to my desk before anybody starts wondering..."

I nod but don't say anything. She rises and walks to the door. I know women. I've spent enough of my time around them; different personalities, different attitudes, but one thing is a universal to all of them. Even my mother. It isn't so much as a look or a facial expression as it is about their posture, even subconsciously. As if intentionally and emotionally distancing themselves from something they don't want to accept. It's as if a wall descends around them. While Ashley's face doesn't betrayed any emotion, I've seen something in her demeanor change.

I frown as she quietly leaves my office, shutting the door softly behind her. Surely, she understands the boundaries of our relationship, doesn't she? Especially since she experienced my playroom. I made the boundaries clear to her, didn't I?

If she didn't understand them, then and now, it isn't my fault. Still, I want to... what? What am I going to do? I'm engaged to Karen Queen, and that isn't going to change anytime soon. Ashley and I can still see each other; that won't change. I don't feel guilty about that, not one iota. Karen and I don't love one another. That too, is plainly understood. Our marriage is simply one of convenience.

Still—

My phone rings again, and I glance down at it then roll my eyes as I answered, "Hello, Mother."

"Daniel." Her voice sounds like it's far away.

"Where are you?"

"On my way down to see the caterer," she says.

Did Karen call my mother to complain, to tell her I'm not invested enough in the wedding planning? "What's up?"

"I know you're busy with your publishing business and everything, Daniel, but really, you could at least pretend you're interested."

I barely hold back a sigh. "Mom, I've done everything she's asked. Yes, I missed the cake tasting appointment last night, but to be brutally honest, I don't care what kind of cake we have. I don't care about the frosting, or the decorations, or what kind of flowers are picked out. Why does this have to be so complicated?"

"These things are important to women," she says, her tone voicing disapproval. "Now I certainly don't expect you to do everything, but to be honest, I think you're being rather rude. I'm trying to help out, but I think you need to do a few things, too."

"She just called, by the way, which I'm sure you know, and I told her I would take care of some phone calls to find a venue for the reception. What else do you need me to do?"

"Shrimp, chicken, or sirloin?"

I space. "What?"

"For the wedding guests. Choose one. Shrimp, chicken, or sirloin?"

I blink. "Why do we have to choose one? Why can't we offer all three? You and I have both been to enough awards and dinners. Why not offer our guests a choice?"

Nothing for several seconds. Did I lose the call? Then I hear her soft laughter.

"There are times, Daniel, when you surprise me. Thank you."

The call disconnects. I lower the phone and stare at it a second. When is this madness going to end? Then, with a sense of frustration, I realize that it probably never will. This is my destiny? To put up or shut up? I sit back in my chair, staring at the manuscripts on my desk, wishing that I could just dive into them, but one image keeps appearing in my mind. One face. It isn't Karen's.

18

ASHLEY

Fiancée. Fiancée. Fiancée... the word reverberates through my brain. With my body still tingling from the sex we just had in his office, I sit down at my desk, placing the manuscript down next to my keyboard, fidgeting with its edges.

"Everything okay?"

I glance up, startled by Tory's question. Her desk only a few feet from mine, I nod. "Why?"

"You look pale."

"I do?" I don't feel pale. I feel like I'm burning alive from the inside out. My unquenched desire has disappeared. It doesn't matter... it doesn't matter! I keep telling myself that, but deep in my gut and in the logical part of my brain, I realize that his words struck a chord, but I shake it off. It's not like we're in a legitimate relationship. It's not like we're officially dating or anything like that. What we do, we do in secret, and I want to keep it that way. What business is it of mine that he has a fiancée?

"Is there something wrong with that manuscript? Does he want you to revise it?"

I glance at Tory, trying to track our sort-of conversation. "Just a couple of things to check over. No worries," I say.

I try to focus my attention back to my computer screen, effectively shutting down any further questions. Nevertheless, I feel Tory's eyes on me. I can tell when she wants more information. After all, I've known her for about as long as I've known Stewart. As his cousin, Tory is the one who introduced us. While our relationship is sort of friendly at work, it isn't like she's my confidant or anything. I don't have any confidantes. No besties, no BFFs, no joined-at-the-hip friends for me. No sir. I'm too busy... too busy focusing on my career aspirations. But man, at this moment, I wish I did have someone to confide in.

Despite my foray into the bondage world, I have to admit to myself that my attitudes, to some degree at least, are traditional. Daniel is engaged. Does his fiancée know about his... his hobby? His underground lifestyle? His many partners and the subs, including me? Maybe she does and maybe she doesn't. It's none of my business. It's theirs. And if she doesn't know, maybe she's better off that way.

Still, I can't help the train of thoughts twisting my insides. What does that make me? And what does it say about Daniel? Then again, is that any of my business either? I shake my head and try to distance myself from thoughts of morality, ethics, and relationships. I stare at the computer screen in front of me, but a myriad of questions keep flipping through my brain, over and over again. The more I think about it, the more I realize I'm in a dead-end situation. Much as I like Daniel, as much as I want to spend more time with him, and even despite my growing feelings for him, I realize that nothing will come of our relationship.

An overwhelming feeling of sadness comes over me. Before I start to wallow in a pool of self-pity, I mentally slap myself. What's wrong with you? I'm not a character in my own manuscript. I'm not a character in any of the romance novels I've edited. For crying out loud, this is real life. It's one thing to have goals and aspirations, another to fool yourself to the point where you believe that fantasy can become reality. Maybe for some people it does, but not for me, not Ashley Shiels.

My hands settle on my keyboard. I remind myself of my own goals, which is to become a published author. Daniel promised that he would publish my manuscript, but where do I go from there? Would I have had the same opportunity to get published if I didn't work here at Pen & Quill? Was he patronizing me, promising to publish my manuscript if... no, don't go there. I think I know Daniel well enough to know that if he thought my manuscript was crap, he would've told me that. Honestly, like any good editor should. Maybe not in those words, but he told me it was good and it just needed a little polishing.

My mind is spinning. I sense Tory occasionally glancing at me, and I finally turn to her with a frown. "What is it? Why do you keep staring at me?"

She says nothing, but merely glances at my computer screen and then back at me. I look at the computer screen and realize I haven't edited one line since I sat down. I come up with an excuse. "Okay, so the manuscript needs a little more work than I implied."

"He's not mad, is he?" She glances down the hall to Daniel's office and lowers her voice. "He can be a prick sometimes, can't he?"

An unreasonable surge of annoyance floods through me, but I quickly tamp it down and offer a lame shrug in reply before again staring at my monitor. Really focused. But I still can't concentrate. Giving up on the computer, I move my keyboard aside and place the proof of the manuscript in front of me and start idly leafing through it. I don't have to do anything with it, it's just a prop, but I pretend to read through it, if just to keep Tory off my case.

Fiancée. Fiancée. Fiancée. A hollow, achy feeling develops in the pit of my stomach. Why do I care? Besides, I have Stewart, don't I? I grimace but then realize that I have to be sensible. Rational. I pull my desk drawer open, pull out my purse and set it on my lap as I dig inside for my phone. Before I can second-guess myself, I text Stewart and ask if he wants to come over tonight.

"Are you sure you're okay?"

I glance at Tory and sigh. "Everything is fine, Tory. I promise."

She finally seems to accept my response and returns to her work. I glance at her occasionally, but she's now fully involved in editing the manuscript on her computer screen. I lied. Everything is not fine. Of course, I wish things had gone differently... I realize where my thoughts were headed. This has to end. Much as I don't want it to, I also don't want to be anyone's mistress, either by implication or the true meaning of the word. Daniel is engaged. That makes everything different.

For the next hour or so I try my best to do the job I'm paid to do, but every few minutes, I find myself glancing down the hallway toward Daniel's office. My emotions range from disappointment to irritation. Why didn't he tell me that he's engaged? Why?

And despite my fantasizing about him for so long, do I really want to be with a man who would cheat so willingly with me and possibly other women? No, no possibly about it. That playroom in his basement is not brand-spanking new, no pun intended. How many subs does he have? How often does he bring them to his secret basement?

I mentally slap myself again. What does it matter? Why should I care? Why did I think that something would come out of our... whatever we're doing? Playtime. That's all it is to Daniel. Getting his rocks off. Playing around. Fucking.

And me? Honestly, what did I expect? It's obvious

to me now that Daniel isn't, and never will be, a one-woman man. For all I know, his fiancée has been down in that playroom as well, and maybe he's had a ménage a trois going on down there, or even orgies. What the hell do I know?

I sigh again, staring at the hallway. When he comes out, I'll give him a look, maybe gesture with my chin for him to meet me out in the hallway outside the office. Or maybe I can manage to time it so that we end up in the elevator alone at the same time. I need to tell him that this is over.

Over before it really even got started. How depressing. The story of my life, isn't it?

I sigh. It was a good experience, and I learned a lot even in a few short sessions. I enjoyed it, no matter how things ended. But it's time to end it. Time to move on.

I don't want to. I want Daniel.

19

ASHLEY

I glance around my apartment, making sure I picked up all the laundry, emptied the trash, and the kitchen sink is clean. Stewart will be here any minute. I cheated and stopped off on the way home from work to pick up Chinese takeout, which is now warming up in a skillet and a pot on my stovetop, the containers in the trash.

I didn't see Daniel emerge from his office, not once, before I left work at five o'clock. Now, close to seven, I'm waiting for Stewart, but not in a good way. I feel like I'm settling, like I'm surrendering, giving up, throwing in the towel. Whatever you want to call it, I'm doing it. I try to be more excited about Stewart's impending arrival. After all, until I started my manuscript and began to fantasize about Daniel and I in that manuscript, I was okay with Stewart, if never sexually satisfied.

Sure, he could be dorky at times, obtuse, and downright annoying. As a pathologist, his world is one of order. Constancy. While the sex is bland, we got along well enough for the most part. I think under different circumstances, we would've been more compatible, but I spent months, if not longer, constantly and mentally comparing Stewart with Daniel. Well shit, Daniel is off the table, so to speak. Now I have to move on. Even so, I find it difficult to work up the same anticipation for seeing Stewart that I experienced with Daniel.

Then again, Daniel and I didn't date, not in the traditional sense of the word. Our interactions were purely sexual in nature. That's obvious by the fact that I didn't even know he was engaged. I know very little about Daniel's day-to-day life, other than what he had divulged in snippets. It's not like we openly went out to dinner, or events, so what the hell?

The knock on my door startles me from my increasing myriad of depressing thoughts. I stare at it for several moments, wondering what Stewart will do if I don't answer. If I pretend I'm not home. No, I can't do that to him.

I move to the door and open it, forcing a small smile. He's wearing an off-the-rack suit from a retail store, his tie crooked, his collar open. "Hey, Stewart." He steps inside, wraps me in his arms, and plants one on my lips. I return the kiss half-heartedly, gently pushing against his shoulders, giving him a small chuckle as I shut the door behind him.

"You hungry?"

"Sure, what are you fixing?"

I gesture toward my small kitchen table. "Chinese takeout."

He chuckles, the one thing about him that I really like. He isn't fussy, that's for sure. He will eat anything that's put in front of him. "Wine?"

"You bet," he says, slipping off his jacket and tossing it over the back of the couch and then heading for the kitchen table.

He pulls up a chair and sits down, crossing one leg over the other as he leans back, one arm dangling over at the back, and looks at me. He has a weird expression on his face; the same look he gets when he's looking through his microscope, studying some bacteria or something.

"What is it?" I finally ask, moving past him into the kitchen to grab a bottle of Merlot and a corkscrew. He turns his head and glances at me over his shoulder. "Spill," I order.

He shrugs. "I admit I was a little surprised that you texted me and wanted me to come over for dinner. You've been avoiding me lately."

The heat of a flush rises in my cheeks, and quickly I lower my head, pretending to concentrate on inserting the corkscrew just so into the wine cork. "It's just been hectic at the office now that the holidays are over, that's all."

He says nothing, and I pour a couple of glasses of Merlot, take them to the table, and sit down across from him. One thing about Stewart; we don't have to fill the silence with empty talk. I sip, and then, watching him gulp down his glass, take a couple larger sips myself before returning to the kitchen, grabbing the bottle, and plunking it down in the middle of the table. He refills both our glasses while I grab a couple plates from the kitchen cupboard and dish up rice and orange cashew chicken.

By the time we finish eating, muttering inane pleasantries throughout supper, I've downed three glasses of wine. My head feels like a balloon floating a short distance from my shoulders. He looks at me and grins.

"How about a romp?"

I shrug. Why the hell not? Without another word, he heads for my bedroom, pulling off his button-down shirt as he makes his way down my short hallway. He's the Stewart I've always known; athletic build, more suited to a surfer than a pathologist. I imagine another relatively tame episode in bed, although he does tend to get a little wild when he drinks wine, which certainly isn't often. His idea of wild is doing it slightly different than the traditional missionary position. Maybe on our sides. Big whoop.

For the first time in a long while, I assess him. His shaggy, not quite brown hair is a bit on the long side, and he has nice-looking green eyes that bespeak an Irish heritage. Come to think of it, he and Daniel are only a couple years apart; Stewart a couple years younger. Stewart's green eyes are more the color of grass, and I automatically compare them to Daniel's bright green. Dammit! Is this to be my fate? Comparing every man I sleep with in the future to Daniel? What if—oomph!

I startle, realizing that Stewart has stopped just in front of my bedroom. I slam into his bare chest as he chuckles, his hands reaching to steady my shoulders. His breath feels warm against my face, smelling of Merlot.

"I forgot condoms."

Nothing like a cold splash of water on my face. I glance up at him, nibbling my lip. "I think there's still a couple in the bathroom cabinet. Go look."

He scooches past me in the hallway and disappears into the bathroom. The light clicks on and I hear the medicine cabinet open and him rustling inside it as I make my way into my bedroom. I pull off my shirt and pants and then climb into bed, slightly dizzy, my thoughts fuzzy.

Moments later, Stewart returns, holding up a red package in his hand. "Found one!" He laugh. "We'll get one shot at this, so we better make it good!"

I watch as he undresses. His cock is already engorged. Try as I might not to, I see Daniel in my mind's eye, making mental comparisons. I purposely shove those thoughts out of my head as Stewart climbs into bed beside me. Leaning his face toward mine, he kisses me, sticking his tongue in my mouth as his hand begins to grope my breast. Then that hand strays downward toward my legs.

I reach for his hand and stop it by the time he gets to my hip. I feel horrible. I want to cry. I want to scream. He doesn't seem to notice, but just keeps kissing and kneading my hip like it's a lump of dough. His cock presses against my thigh.

It's at this moment I realize I can't go through with this. I'm just not into it. I can't get Daniel out of my head. I don't want to have boring sex with Stewart. To even suggest something a little different will really upset the status quo, at least as far as Stewart is concerned. I can't really fault him for it. It's just that sex with Stewart is dull. Always the same. It was boring before I experienced bondage with Daniel.

I pull away from him, and although I still feel a little fuzzy, I know what I need to do. He tries to envelope me in his grasp, and I place my hand on his chest. He looks at me, his pupils slightly dilated, his lips open, his face flushed.

"What is it? You want to put it on?"

For a second I don't know what he's talking about until he extends the still rolled condom toward me. "No, Stewart, I don't want to put it on—"

"You want to go bareback?"

I stare, dismayed that he even knows the term. "No, I don't want to go bareback, either. Stewart, I can't do this."

"What do you mean?" He frowns, and then his eyes widen. "You're not on your period, are you?"

Oh my God. "No, Stewart, I'm not on my period. I just can't do this." He reaches for me again, and I pull away even more. Another inch and I'll fall out of the bed. I lift myself onto my elbow, one hand placed firmly on his chest. "I mean I can't do this. Sex. Us."

"What are you saying, Ashley?" He gestures at the bed. "We're lying naked in your bed. And you just changed your mind?"

I don't want to hurt him, really I don't. I steel myself and rolled out of bed, quickly heading for my dresser, where I yank out a T-shirt and a pair of sweatpants. He watches me pull them on, his expression confused.

"Ashley, what's going on? Did I say something? What?"

Do it, I tell myself. Do it now. Cut the cord. Quickly. I have his full attention now. He sits up in bed, staring at me. "I don't want to hurt you, Stewart, but I just don't think it's fair for either one of us to continue. I—"

"Is it that guy at work? Your boss?"

My mouth drops open and I deny it. "It's not, Stewart," I say. That at least is the truth. "I just need some time to figure out where I am and what I want."

He sits up, swinging his legs over the side of the bed, reaching for his trousers. "And you waited until we're in bed to tell me this?"

"I'm sorry, Stewart, I didn't realize that... that it was over between us until we got into the bed."

He frowns. "I don't believe it. You met another guy." He jerks his pants on, his movements stiff and awkward. "Why didn't you just tell me? Why string me along? How long have you been stringing me along, Ashley?"

"I didn't do it deliberately, Stewart," I say, crossing my arms over my chest. Even I realize it's a self-defense mechanism. "I just don't feel like I can commit to a relationship, not the way you want me to. We're at different places in our goals. So, what's the point? I don't want to just have casual sex. You can understand that, can't you?"

He mumbles something that I can't understand. I don't bother to ask him to repeat it. It doesn't matter. He steps toward the bedroom door and then leans down to snatch his shirt from the floor. He pauses, then slowly threads his arms through the sleeves, every move precise, straining for what I perceive as his attempt to maintain his dignity. His face flushes with emotion as he looks at me, enclosing the buttons on his shirt. He rubs a hand through his hair and lowers his eyebrows. His eyes bore into mine, it's as if he can read every thought racing through my head.

"I'm sorry, Stewart, I don't—"

He lifts a hand. "You do know, Ashley, that once I walk out of here, it's over. Forever. I'm not going to beg. I'm not going to take you back. It's obvious to me that you've already decided." He shakes his head. "But I'll say one thing. I thought we were in a relationship. I thought we were on the same page. The least you could have done is have the decency to talk to me about this." He shakes his head again and then turns and leaves the room.

I don't move, not even after I hear the front door open and close softly behind him. The apartment grows still. I gaze at the bed, my clothes on the floor, and then, out of nowhere, my eyes fill with tears and a stifled sob erupts from my throat.

Shit.

20

DANIEL

I sequester myself in my office for the rest of the day, trying to deal with business though my mind refuses to focus, constantly revolving around Ashley, Karen, and my mother to the point that I finally give up, lean back in my chair, and close my eyes in an attempt to block all of it out, if even for a minute or two. I keep thinking about the expression on Ashley's face when I told her about Karen. It was brief, but I saw the slight widening of her eyes, that almost flinch. She walked out of my office, head lowered, but with a straight spine and squared shoulders. She was almost as good as I was at hiding emotion.

The problem I have to resolve now, that's been bouncing in my brain since the moment the door shut behind her is, do I care? The simple answer is yes. Ashley was certainly inexperienced with bondage, but she's eager to learn. She's a natural when it comes to quickly adapting to different ways of doing things in my playroom. We clicked. I grimace as the word forms in my brain. Another stupid cliché, but hell, if the word fit, the word fit. The truth is, I want more from her than that.

"What the hell are you getting at?" I mutter into the silence of my office. I know that if I put the answer into words, it will change everything, and not necessarily for the better.

I know everything I want to know about Karen, which isn't much, mostly superficial, but I have no real desire to learn more. Our conversations don't delve deep beneath the surface into emotions and feelings. It's not like we're in love, after all. And why should it matter anyway? Our marriage, quite simply, is a matter of convenience, at least as far as I'm concerned. I got the impression that Karen feels much the same way.

On the other hand, I *do* want to get to know Ashley better. It's not just that sex with her is easy, in terms of it feeling so natural and relaxing. Even in the height of a session, I felt tension and anxiety leaving my body, replaced by sensations of, if not joy, then close to it. In just a few sessions, she already learned to anticipate what I wanted and what I needed. We're well matched. Nevertheless, I still can't put my finger exactly on what it is that attracts me to Ashley. She should've been just another sub, but she isn't.

Do I need to analyze this? Isn't it enough to experience those rare emotions of serenity that I feel around her? I cringe as I find my thoughts turning maudlin. My thoughts sound corny, even to myself, like something out of one of the manuscripts that often cross my desk, but for the first time in my life, I understand it.

I'm supposed to meet Karen after work, to deal with some of the wedding stuff, and I'm not looking forward to it. Lately, it seems every time I turn around, my mother or Karen want something from me. I'm tired of doing all the giving, of keeping everyone happy. Except myself, that is. Before Ashley came along, before I glanced at her laptop, I was resigned, if not completely satisfied to do what my mother wanted, mainly because I knew that I would be able to continue the enjoyment of my secret and keep my life pretty much the way it was. I doubted that Karen and I would spend much social time together, which was perfectly fine with me and probably fine with her as well.

I pick up a pen and idly tap it against my blotter, frowning, my lips pursed. Dammit. I'd been going through the motions before I met Ashley. Now, everything has changed. I want more. I *need* more. I didn't really realize it until now. I also realize something else, and when I do, a knot settles in the pit of my stomach.

I have to do something about it.

For the first time in my life, I know what I want, above and beyond work goals and the enjoyable yet temporary release I gain from my subs. I want to get to know a real woman. A woman like Ashley; more than as my sub, more than as my employee. I want to spend time with her aboveground, dating. Traditionally dating. But if I break off the engagement with Karen, my mother will be scandalized. No doubt about it. She even might go so far as to request the board of directors to undercut me at our family company, but do I really care? Sure, she would do so quietly. Nothing so crass as my mother airing her dirty laundry in public would do. What Karen or her family will do, I don't know, and I don't particularly care.

Even if I'm voted off the board of directors of the family business, I'll be all right. My heart is with my publishing company, and I have enough money that I don't need to lean on the family business for my survival. The more I think about it, the more I realize that it's time. Time to make some changes. Time to change the way I do things.

I don't want to marry Karen. I'm not attracted to her, and I don't even particularly care for her. I definitely don't like spending time with her. Having sex with Karen isn't enjoyable either, though it isn't her fault she isn't experienced enough to know what I want, what I need, nor how to please me. Karen thinks of sex as black or white, nothing in between. She only does traditional things, safe and plain and vanilla. She refuses to give or get oral sex. She refuses to push the boundaries and experiment once in a while. I've tried to encourage her, just once, to let herself cut loose and let me suck on her pussy as she sucked on my dick, and she shut down. Told me that only perverted people do things like that.

And so, I sit in my office, scowling at my dark computer screen, not exactly waffling, but weighing the pros and cons. I could break things off with Karen, but I already told Ashley that our relationship is purely sexual, purely related to me as her Dom and she as my sub. Does she want more?

I have a feeling she will, considering how her characters developed in her manuscript. Those characters were more than just lovers. They were partners. Soulmates. Again, I grimace and shake my head. I'm getting carried away. Besides, Ashley might not even want me for more than a sexual partner. Still, even those considerations don't really change anything. I don't want to marry Karen. The thought of pursuing Ashley is beside the point.

Heaving a heavy sigh, I finally pick up my phone, stare at it for several moments, and then bring up my contact list. I scroll down to Karen's name. It has to be done. I try to convince myself that doing this is for both our sakes, but I don't believe that Karen will feel the same way. She doesn't care whether she loves me or not. I'm a good catch by any standards. She and her family would undoubtedly be upset if the marriage fell apart. After all, they need capital. I grunt a chortle. Will my mother offer them a deal? Severance pay? I might be cutting off my nose to spite my face, but I see no other alternative. The thought of spending the rest of my life, let alone the near future, with Karen is unacceptable.

I'm grown man. I don't need my mother's permission or approval to do anything. I press the speed dial and hear Karen's phone ringtone on the other end. Unanswered, my call goes to voicemail.

"Karen, we need to talk."

"NO! YOU CAN'T DO THIS!"

I sit in a corner of the sofa in my penthouse suite, trying to maintain a bland expression. I'm not cold-hearted, but I know I can't respond to Karen's growing histrionics. She paces from one side of the room to the other, her face red, flinging her hands this way and that, pausing only occasionally to glare at me. A few times she actually sputters, struggling to find words.

I know that my announcement that I was breaking off our engagement shocked her. Her reaction, her mouth dropping open, her hand touching her chest, and the chuckle of laughter in her throat when she thought I was joking slowly morphed into red cheeks, narrowed eyes, and literally bared teeth.

"What the hell has gotten into you?" she demands.

She pauses in front of the expansive window overlooking the city and then turns to look at me, arms crossed over her chest.

"You know that our parents have gone to a lot of trouble to arrange this—"

"You don't need to keep reminding me that this is an arranged marriage, Karen," I say. I hoped, foolishly perhaps, that I would give her the news and she would absorb it and then storm out, probably slamming the door loudly behind her. But no, she lingered, as if she thought she could talk me out of it.

"*Why*?"

"You know I don't love you, Karen, and I know you don't love me. So, what's the point? You and I both know that we'll end up making each other miserable. Is that how you want to spend the next year, five years, or the rest of your life?"

She gives a dismissive gesture. "My mother told me that she and my dad didn't love each other when they got married, but they grew to love each other over the years. Now they're practically inseparable."

And miserable. I've seen Karen's parents on occasion, only to note their obvious disdain for one another. They barely look at each other, their conversations short and clipped, their body language—to me, at least—clarifying also that they no longer share a bed. Still, Karen is playing the part of jilted fiancée to the hilt, pretending that she cares about me when I know she doesn't.

"I'm sorry, Karen, but this isn't going to work, and I don't think it's fair—"

"Fair?"

Her voice cracks as she takes a step toward me, hands balled into fists.

"*Fair*? You're waiting until I'm deciding on wedding cake flavors and floral arrangements to tell me that you've changed your mind? And how is that fair?" She pauses and sucks in a breath. "Why are you being such a fucking bastard?"

I've been waiting for Karen's true nature to show. The fake tears are gone and the banshee is out. Her eyes narrow on me, her jaw clenches, a visible vein throbbing in her neck. An almost feral growl rumbles upward from deep in her chest, but to her credit, she doesn't let it loose. She stares down at the floor a moment, then looks back at me. Another cliché captures my thoughts—if looks could kill, I'd be dead by now.

I don't want to hurt her, but I can't cave. I can't allow those crocodile tears shining in her eyes to sway me. She isn't furious because she can't have *me*. She's furious because... well, who the hell knows what she actually thinks.

"Don't you think our parents will have something to say about this?" she hisses.

"I frankly don't care," I say. "I shouldn't have waited so long, Karen, I know, and for that I do apologize. But I thought as time went by, as the wedding got closer, I would begin to feel differently. But the brutally honest truth is, I don't. I just don't think we can make a happy marriage of it. So again, what's the point?"

She takes several more steps toward me. I don't move. Perhaps she'll slap me, and I'll probably let her. But only one. No more than that. She doesn't. She stops and a look of pure vitriol crosses her features. Her lips turn down in a snarl.

"You're going to regret this, Daniel."

I say nothing. I probably won't, at least for a while. In fact, my mother just might not ever forgive me, but I figure she'll come around eventually. This entire arrangement has been ill advised from the start, but wanting to please her, I went along with it.

I should've known better. The plain truth of the matter is, if Ashley didn't come along when she did, I might have.

21

ASHLEY

I sit in my apartment at the kitchen table, my laptop open in front of me, the blank screen of the new Word document daring me to write something. The curser waits patiently. I haven't heard from Daniel since I was in his office bent over his desk, my legs held apart by the spreader bar. He didn't tell me in so many words that we were over, and I haven't spoken the words to him, but the moment he told me about his engagement, things changed. For me at least. He's made no effort to text me, to send me a note, to call me back into his office, nothing.

It's over.

In fact, I haven't seen him in the publishing house since I left his office, closing the door softly behind me. I didn't dare ask anyone if they've seen him. He's probably just off on another of his business trips. Then again, maybe he's gone off to get married to Karen. I don't know anything about their arrangements or their upcoming wedding date. The thought depresses me, but not to the degree where I allow myself to wallow in self-pity. It does bug me, no doubt about that, but I'm not despondent, not lying in my bed crying my eyes out, thinking that my life is over.

I know that my fling with Daniel was merely an interlude in his life. Maybe it meant more to me than it did to him, but I'm not naïve. I can live with my unrequited affection for him. I can continue to work for him, too. It might be awkward at first, but it will just take a little bit of time. Maybe a long time. Every time I think of him, I think of what we did in his office the last time we were together. Just the thought of it makes my heart skip a beat. My gaze keeps drifting from my laptop toward the window, my thoughts continually drifting back to him. Daniel.

Problem is, I've ignored the truth for too long. *Go ahead and say it*, my brain orders. Okay, I love him. I love Daniel. Maybe I've loved him all this time. Maybe using him as a foundation for the character in my book, the one in which I romped happily ever after with him, in my manuscript was merely my way of subconsciously recognizing my feelings.

Stupid of me, really, thinking that I, Ashley Shiels, could have my cake and eat it, too. I'm not usually prone to such negative thoughts, but I have to be honest with myself for a change. I've been a fool.

Live and learn.

I sigh, shut down my laptop, and close it, knowing that I'm not going to get any more work done on it this evening. I meander into the kitchen, thinking to make some tea when I hear the quiet knock on my door. I frown, glancing at the clock on the stove. Nine-thirty. Who the hell—Stewart. It's been a few days since I've heard from him, giving him enough time to work up a reaction, an attempt to talk me out of my decision. That's Stewart. When we got into an argument, it usually took him seventy-two hours to process and come back with a retort. I've timed it, many times. Seventy-two hours; no more and no less.

Setting the box of tea bags back onto the counter, I sigh and stride toward my door, rehearsing what to say to him when I open it. I'm not going to let him in. I'm not going to give him the opportunity to start an argument. I don't have the energy. When I open the front door, you could knock me over with a feather.

Not Stewart, but Daniel. I stare at him, eyes wide, my mouth open in surprise.

"We're not done yet."

He steps into the apartment and I let him, and then cast a quick glance around, hoping I didn't leave any clothes on the floor or dirty dishes in the sink. I'm not exactly compulsive about cleaning.

"How did you know where I live?"

He walks to my couch, calm as anything, and sits down, crossing his legs and extending one arm along the back of it. Making himself right at home.

"It's on your application file."

God, that's a stupid question. I close the door and then turn to face him, just standing there like an idiot, staring at him in dismay. "What about your fiancée?" I shake my head. "I can't say that I haven't enjoyed our time together, Daniel, but I'm a bit of a traditionalist in—"

"I broke it off with her," he interrupts.

I'm rendered completely speechless. I stare at him for several moments, thinking that he's joking. He has to be. "You what?" My stomach doesn't flip-flop. What's he talking about? What's he saying? What is he *not* saying?

"I broke off the engagement," he says simply.

I stared, aghast. "But why?" How could he do that? From what I gathered, they were in the final stages of wedding planning. Did he do it for me? I nearly choke. And then tell myself I'm an idiot again. He wouldn't break off his engagement for me. Idiot. He told me that our relationship was to have no strings, so what is he intimating? I'm getting ahead of myself, I have to be. No, he didn't break off his engagement because of me. Did he? I shake my head. "I don't understand."

"It was an arrangement, Ashley. I don't love her, and I sure as hell don't believe that she loves me. So, I broke it off."

He states it so simply, without any emotion whatso-ever. Okay, so—

"Ashley, I would like to try taking our relationship to a different level."

I stand, my brain not tracking his words. "What?"

He pats the couch cushion beside him. "Come sit down. Let me explain."

Slowly, I approach the couch and sit down next to him. Tonight is the time for firsts, isn't it? The first time he's been in my apartment. The first time I sat next to him, on a couch no less, with my clothes on, in a different kind of situation. He feels comfortable, no doubt about it, but I don't know what to do. Is he my Dom now or is—

"Up until this point in time, we've had a Dom/sub relationship, Ashley. But I would like to suggest a bit of a change."

He sits so close I feel the heat emanating from his body. For the first time—another first—I feel that we're talking more as a couple, like friends—with benefits, yes, but on an equal level. "I'm not sure I understand," I say softly. I sure as hell don't.

"I want to spend more time with you." He shrugs. "Spend more time other than just in my playroom."

I can't imagine what my face looks like. Inside, I feel breathless. My entire body tenses and for a second. Did I hear correctly? Is he telling me that he wants to—

His face leans toward mine and then his lips are on mine, kissing gently, softly nibbling, and then deepening in pressure. His tongue traces a path around my lower lip and then urges my mouth open. My heart pounds. Of course, I open my mouth to him, not quite certain what—

His breath feels warm against my lips. I say nothing. What can I say? My body tingles all over as I try to absorb what he's saying. But it's so hard to concentrate with his tongue doing that curling thing with mine. Is he saying that he wants to date me? Or that he doesn't want to do that Dom/sub thing anymore? I don't understand. I can't grasp this sudden change, but my questions will have to wait. As his lips increase their pressure on mine, I feel a surge of joy bubble up inside me. We're acting like a normal couple would, sitting on the couch, kissing. I can't believe it. Needless to say, one thing leads to another. His hand slips up underneath the hem of my shirt and his hand leaves a trail of heat on my skin as he skims it along my side and then cups my breast. His thumb circles my nipple. At first, I'm not quite sure what to do. Did we slip back into the Dom/sub roll? He isn't acting like it but... do I have to wait for permission to touch him? I break off the kiss and slowly lift my head, raising an eyebrow in silent question. His hand and fingers pause in their achingly tender stroking.

"Tonight, Ashley, I'm not your Dom. You're not my sub. Let's just see how it goes, shall we?"

My mind is still spinning, trying to ascertain what he means by a change. Certainly, he isn't suggesting that we... but his hand is so warm, so gentle, caressing my breast in a way he's never done before. Before, our encounters in the playroom were a bit more... intense? Desperate? Hurried? No, not desperate, but propelled by the incitement of his gadgets, the unknown.

I place my palms against his chest, reveling in the breadth of his pecs, marveling that tonight, we will be lovers. Not playing a role, just enjoying each other's body, no rules, no tools and gadgets, just the two of us. And I know that even without any tools, having sex with Daniel won't be dull in the least. My nipples harden and extend, as if begging for his touch on their own. My pulse races, and the heat of desire tingles through my body. I'm anxious to explore this new side of Daniel; this side of him that I've never seen before. He leans back and so do I, both of us staring at one another.

I'm still not sure what this means. I'm certainly not going to jump to any conclusions. While I have to admit that I'm a bit disappointed that we won't be using any toys, based on how I'm feeling already, we don't need them, at least not tonight.

"Shall we take this into the bedroom?"

I moisten my lips, enjoying the sight of his gaze dipping to my mouth. His pulse races too, I can tell by the throbbing of the vein along the side of his neck. It gives me a thrill to know that I can trigger such a response in him without the gadgets.

I nod.

In my bedroom, he undresses me, though I only wore a pair of sweats, a T-shirt, sans bra, and my underwear. In seconds, I stand naked before him. Slowly, I undress him. My fingers tremble only slightly as I unbutton his shirt, then peel it off his broad shoulders. I keep my eyes on him while I unbuckle his belt, then unzip his pants. I tuck my hands inside the waistband and slide the trousers past his hips. Then his boxers.

His cock is hard already, pointing at me. I look at it and it moves of its own accord, as if trying to touch me. I grasp his cock in my palm as he slides his feet from his shoes and then kicks his pants and boxers away. He doesn't move after that, keeps his hands down by his sides while I take advantage. My hands are everywhere; trailing along those strong shoulders, across his chest, my palms circling his nipples into hard little nubs.

I grow wet between my legs. My hands skim along his hips and then along the outside of his muscular thighs. Abruptly, I sit down on the bed, then grasp his ass and urge him closer to me as I take him into my mouth. My tongue twirls around his head, eliciting a drop of moisture. One hand grasping his cock, the other cups his balls, gently massaging, squeezing and then releasing. I tease as my tongue does a number along his shaft, while my other hand grasps his ass, contracted into a hard mass. God, he is beautiful.

I suckle his head, and then urge him a little deeper, my tongue circling his head, then his shaft, then sucking hard two or three times before I repeat the process. I thrill when I hear him hiss in a breath. His hands grasp my shoulders and then he pushes me back onto the bed. He nestles himself between my legs and pushes against my ankles until my knees are bent, opening myself to him.

My hands on his shoulders, his groping my breasts, he slides down until his mouth finds my mound. Then my nub. I groan and throw my head back, reveling in the sensations that rush through my body.

I'm so wet and hot for him I rock my hips upward. "Please... Daniel... I need you—"

He chuckles, and I feel it jolt through my body. My head is pounding, my body pounding, my blood pounding. He makes me feel with every nerve ending, every sensation more glorious than the last. This is heaven.

He shifts his position and I feel bereft, but he's back in a second, holding onto a condom wrapper.

"You do it."

He hands it to me. I take it, not the least embarrassed that my legs are splayed before him. I rip open the package as he stares at my pussy with a smile. My hands tremble as I retrieve the circle of latex. He leans forward, his knees inside mine and his weight balanced on his hands, placed on either side of my shoulders. I place the condom on his head and slowly roll it down while he watches my face, that smile playing around his mouth wanting me to forego the condom and just shove him deep inside me.

The moment the condom is in place, he repositions himself. He lifts my hips again with his arms and finds my entrance with his shaft. He enters me slowly—excruciatingly slowly, as if by one centimeter at a time. My pussy contracts around him, urging him forward. I breathe hard, the anticipation nearly killing me. Then, with a chuckle, his jaw tight with tension, he lunges forward, his cock filling me. I marvel again that his huge shaft can fit inside me.

"Watch."

The word is spoken gently, but with command. I gaze at his face, see the tension as he holds himself still, and then I do as he asked. I stare down at our union. I see that he's buried himself nearly to the hilt. He slowly retreats, pulling his length from my pussy as slowly as he entered. I stare in fascination. His cock glistens with my juices, the veins raised and pulsing, the shaft itself a pinkish color—I groan, grab his ass with both my hands, lift my legs and wrap them around his waist and then pull him deeper.

He laughs and allows me to take the lead, to set the pace. I rock my hips with abandon, enjoying this kind of sex with him as much as I do the bondage. And just before I achieve climax, one image reverberates through my brain.

The look on Daniel's face. His smile.

22

ASHLEY

I lay panting on the bed, Daniel next to me, but my bliss is interrupted by the sound of a phone ring tone. His phone. He reaches over the side of the bed for his clothes and retrieves it. I turn to watch him, admiring the sight of his naked back and the ripple of muscles in his broad shoulders tapering to a narrow waistline. Not an ounce of fat on him anywhere. He's all muscle. Just looking at him, gazing at the flair of his hips and his ass, gets me all hot again. I barely resist the urge to slide my hand between his legs and grope his balls.

"Excuse me," he says, offering a quick glance over his shoulder. "If I don't get it, I can guarantee you the phone will ring every five minutes until I do."

"Go ahead," I murmur, grinning. My body still thrums with the aftermath of our lovemaking—there, I said it. It wasn't just sex. That romp in bed just now was a genuine session of lovemaking, and I felt the difference. This sex was leisurely, gentle, and... exquisite. When we were in the playroom I also enjoyed the sex, but that was more like fucking; it was fast and intense and quick, and this was... this was wonderful.

"I'm busy, Mother, what is it?"

I barely hear the sound of a female voice coming from his phone. He startles me when he sits up abruptly, his back stiff. Even before he says a word I can sense the tension emanating from him.

"What? Are you sure?"

The one-sided conversation continues for a moment, and then Daniel speaks again, his voice low and uncertain. "I did. I called her last night and told her. We both know that it's—yes, I understand, and I know I should have said something sooner, but I—"

I frown as he reaches for his clothes on the floor. I sit up too, holding the sheet to my breasts. Don't ask me why, because Lord knows, Daniel has seen me naked before. Something is wrong.

"All right, I'll be there... I'll get there soon as I can, all right?"

Daniel disconnects the call and sits for several seconds, not moving.

"What is it? What's happened?"

When he turns around to face me, I feel the invisible punch to the gut. Just a moment ago, his face was flushed with exertion, his pupils dilated, his breathing raspy, his grin oh-so-sexy. It was some of the best sex I've ever had, and I hoped he felt the same way—

"It's Karen."

It takes a second for my brain to switch gears. "Karen?" Who is Karen? And then I remember. "Your fiancée... I mean, your ex-fiancée?"

He nods, standing to pull on his boxers. He doesn't look at me. I resist the urge to stare at his now limp dick, knowing that nothing will come of it. He's leaving.

"My mom called to tell me that she's in the hospital."

"Oh my God... what happened?"

"My mom says that she—Karen—called her a while ago, after I broke off the engagement. Karen sounded distraught, but she managed to get her calmed down. Just now, though, she learned that Karen had been admitted to the hospital."

"What happened?" I ask again, my voice faint and shaky. Oh my God, I hope the woman will be all right. When Daniel speaks, I barely recognize his voice.

"She tried to kill herself."

I stare at him, disbelieving. I scramble out of bed, looking for my clothes. "What can I do?"

He shoves his legs into his trousers, slips on his shoes, and then pushes his arms through the sleeves of his dress shirt. His hands shake slightly as he tries to button it. I start to move, to help him, and then freeze, especially when he looks up at me, his expression filled with what I can only construe as guilt. He gives me a look that doesn't need explaining. He mutters softly to himself, tugging at his collar even though it's perfect. He stares down at his feet for a moment, then finally looks up at me.

That look washes all doubt away and triggers a feeling of intense disappointment. I know what he's going to say before he says anything. He stands on one side of the bed, me on the other as he speaks.

"I have to go... you understand that, right?"

I don't answer, and he doesn't give me an opportunity. He continues, speaking quickly, as if he has to get it out all at once. "It's not really Karen's fault that my mom pressured the both of us to get engaged. The engagement was intended to provide benefits for both our families..."

Even before he finishes speaking, I know where this is going. I almost say *no backsies*, but I keep my mouth shut. I'm not going to beg. I'm not going to be weak.

"I have to go to the hospital to make sure she's okay. And I have to make things right. I'm sorry, Ashley, but I have to do the right thing here. I have to do the responsible thing."

I stand frozen, my body still tingling from the sensations those hands of his had invoked deep inside me. I stand naked, grasping the sheet to my body as he turns to leave the room.

He doesn't look back.

I hear the front door open and close, but I still stand there, staring down at the bed, the rumpled sheets, the smell of sex still permeating the room. My brain feels numb. Damn it! I sink down onto the bed, staring out the window, wondering how in the hell I had managed to do this to myself twice.

I got my hopes up, despite my own internal instincts and warnings not to. When he showed up at my door less than two hours ago, my heart leapt with excitement, and even more so when he told me he broke off the engagement. His words gave me hope that not only our 'downstairs' relationship wasn't over; but actually, it was just going to get better. It was validation, for *me* at least, that he did feel something for me, something that went beyond "playtime" and my foray into the world of bondage.

Why did I even feel that way? *Why*? When I first learned that he had a fiancée, I made the decision to give him up. I didn't want that kind of a relationship. I dealt with it, or was beginning to anyway. I made a logical decision to just let it go. You win some, you lose some. But when he showed up at my door... no, that was different. I'm only fooling myself.

Not that he said that he had chose me, no. All he implied was that he had *not* chosen Karen. I still don't expect any promises from Daniel, at least I don't think so, but now, sitting here on my bed, in my room, naked, I find myself growing annoyed. And to be honest, I'm more upset than I was in his office when I first learned of his fiancée because I had—obviously subconsciously—let myself hope. Let myself hope that by his coming here, it might have meant something.

"You're a stupid idiot."

I sigh. I'm bummed. No, I'm depressed. Such an

emotional roller coaster. Who the hell needs it? I'm not heartbroken, and I'm not going to be. I don't need any man in my life to validate who I am or what I want to be. I don't *need* Daniel, and I don't *need* Stewart. Let him have Karen. I don't wish ill on either one of them, and I certainly hope that Karen will be all right, but who needs that kind of drama?

I got my hopes up twice. What's that saying? Fool me once, shame on you. Fool me twice, shame on me? I stand, drop the sheet, and head for the shower. I'm stronger than that. Will I make the same mistake again? Maybe. I don't know. But I know one thing. If Daniel wants to let guilt rule his life, there is nothing I can do about it. I'm not going to be a part of it.

Standing in the shower with the water pouring over me, I feel slightly rejuvenated. I don't cry. Maybe that will come later, I'm not sure. Right now, I tell myself that what I have to do is focus on my own goals, which means getting my book finished and published with or without Daniel's help. And then, someday, I'll find the right man, and then, just maybe, I just might consider settling down.

23

DANIEL

I feel like a son of a bitch for even thinking it, but I can't help it. I'm miserable. It's been a week since I got that phone call at Ashley's place that Karen tried to kill herself. I'd been guilt-ridden, and my mother's trembling voice affected me. I'd never heard her sound like that. I didn't... I didn't know how to feel. I didn't want to be cruel to Karen, but I broke off the engagement with the intention of sparing us both.

Karen apparently tried to overdose on Ambien, at least that's what I was told by the doctor at the hospital. At first, he didn't want to give me any information, stating that I wasn't a family member, but I told him that I was Karen's fiancé and he checked and saw that I was one of her emergency contacts. He gave me the rundown. Apparently, it was Karen herself who'd called 9-1-1. When the paramedics got to her apartment, they found a prescription bottle beside her on the bed. A half glass of Merlot was on the end table beside the bed. I frowned, confused. As far as I knew, Karen didn't take any medication. I just started to talk to the doctor about that when my mother appeared beside me. She clasped my arm tightly, and when I looked down at her, I felt a jolt.

Without her usual impeccable makeup, she looked older, pale, and yes, even frail. All I could think of is that I did this to her. It was the first time I had seen my mother in such an emotional state.

"She's going to be all right," I told her, wrapping an arm around her shoulder, holding her close to me. Her eyes filled with tears as she looked up at the doctor.

She turned to me, her eyes wide. "She sounded so funny when she called me, like she was slurring, but I thought she'd just had one too many. She sounded so drowsy and confused... then she told me she'd called 9-1-1, that she'd taken pills, tried to commit suicide..."

"The doctor said she took some pills and alcohol."

"She doesn't take pills, not even aspirin," she said.

"She's doing fine now," the doctor said. "We performed a gastric lavage, we pumped her stomach, and then gave her flumazenil as a precaution. Her cardiac and respiratory functions are fine. We'll keep her overnight for observation, but she should be able to go home tomorrow."

"But—"

"I would suggest you get her some psychiatric counseling to deal with the issues that triggered the overdose."

"Her parents are traveling abroad for another week—I haven't been able to reach them."

"Does she live alone?"

"Yes," I replied.

"I would suggest that someone stay with her—"

"Daniel can stay with her at her apartment until her parents return."

I was about to object, and strongly, but didn't want to argue in front of the doctor. He simply nodded, and after notifying us that the nurses would keep us updated, he turned and left.

"Mother, I just broke up with her. She's not going to want to—"

"You know she's been under an enormous amount of stress, Daniel. And to just throw that out at her? That you're done?"

She gave me the look; the look she perfected over the years, since I was a teen. One that conveyed sad disappointment. I inhaled, counted to five, and then exhaled. I would give her this one.

"She intimated to me that you'd been seeing someone else, that you must have been because you haven't been particularly interested in... in personal time with her."

I didn't even know how to respond to that without divulging anything about Ashley. "Mother, I am not going to discuss my sex life with you." At the same time, I realized that continuing a relationship with Ashley at this point would be unfair to her.

Upon hearing the news of Karen's hospitalization, my guilt weighed so heavily on me that I decided I *would* take responsibility, that I would try to make things work between us, that I would continue with the plans for marriage. Did I *want* to? No, but I certainly didn't want someone's suicide attempt resting on my shoulders.

That was nearly a week ago. A week during which I realized, once again, that I actually feel stuck between a rock and a hard place. Stuck with a woman I don't care about. Oh, I've done my part, telling her she has to rest in bed the day after she got discharged from the hospital. Tried to show concern, tried to listen to her crying—no tears—about how devastated she was when I broke it off with her, and how she didn't think she could go on.

She didn't seem much worse for the wear to me. She got clingy, fast. Every time I tried to leave her bedroom she started to weep, sniffling into her Kleenex as if it were the end of the world. She was a drama queen before. Now? This was getting ridiculous.

I know one thing that would definitely soothe my own stress and increasing aggravation, but I can't bring myself to look for a random sub to have sex with in my basement. I resolve that I definitely won't call Ashley. Especially not after I told her that I wanted a different relationship with her. She hasn't called and I haven't called her either—not yet, anyway. I don't think she will reach out to me. I will call her, but not until I get everything figured out.

At the moment, I'm in the kitchen of Karen's apartment, preparing soup for lunch. Not really preparing it, just warming it up. She had a shitload of groceries delivered to the apartment a couple of days ago, which I had a feeling was more to keep me in the apartment rather than having me be *inconvenienced*—her words, not mine—by going shopping for groceries on my own.

I need to get the hell out of here, if only for a little while. She's driving me nuts.

"Daniel..."

Speak of the devil. I glance up from the open kitchen area as Karen sweeps into the room in a loose-fitting silk pantsuit. She carries a sheaf of papers with her and brings them to the table in her dining room. Crap. More wedding plans. What now?

Shaking my head, striving for patience, telling myself that I can do this, I dish a serving of soup into a bowl, grab a spoon, and venture from the kitchen into the dining area. Placing the bowl and spoon down on the table, I notice her smiling.

She glances up and reaches for my hand. I can barely tolerate her touch. That's how bad it's gotten. A week straight with Karen has pushed me to the point where I can barely look at her. Is this my future? Last night, she hinted about sex, and I demurred, not even counting on the negative response with an *oh, you're not well enough yet* comment. The fact is, I don't want to have sex with Karen. I don't want to have sex with any of my subs. I want to have sex with Ashley. That's it, bottom line.

Her words startle me, spoken so abruptly.

"I realize that on occasion you see other women, Daniel, but that's all over now. Isn't it?"

Her eyes on mine, I look down at her. I heave a

mental sigh, realizing that I can't say what I truly want to say, at least not yet. Her parents are due back tomorrow. I don't want to leave her alone, afraid that she might attempt another suicide. I hate that she's literally holding me as a mental hostage. I just don't know what to do about it. I feel responsible and disgusted at the same time. If I don't do as she asks, will she threaten a repeat performance? And if she does, what will I do? She did it once, I came to the rescue, so what will prevent her from doing it again?

"This is the way it's going to be, Karen?"

"What? I don't understand." She shrugs and glances at the papers on the table. "What do you think about the seating arrangement your mother helped me with?"

How can she continue to pretend that everything is fine? Seriously? How can she pretend that she's happy about the upcoming wedding, which apparently is on again. Doesn't she understand? Doesn't she comprehend? Resentment flows. I'm not sure if it's the smug smile on her face or the fact that I'm so frustrated, unable to get out of this apartment for even a couple of hours in the past week that has me snapping at her.

"And if I don't like something, or if I do something you don't like, are you going to try and kill yourself again?"

The moment the words are out of my mouth, I regret it. What a horrible thing to say. To my surprise, she merely smiles and turns to look through her paperwork.

"You came back, didn't you?" She waves a hand at me. "Besides, it was only a couple of pills."

It takes several seconds for her words to sink in. I'm rendered speechless. "What?"

She freezes, then glances quickly at me, then back down at her papers. She clears her throat. "All's well that end's well, isn't that right?" She shakes her head. "It was an accident—"

I stiffen. "My mother told me that you said that you wanted to die. Do you remember that, Karen?"

Again, she waves a hand and looks up at me, a pout forming on her lips, blinking rapidly as if she's trying to create tears. "I can't talk about it, Daniel," she says, her voice soft and trembling. "It was... it was just a foolish accident."

I frown down at her. What the hell? I turn and begin to walk away from the table.

"Aren't you going to eat lunch with me?"

"I have to go to the bathroom."

"When you get back, we'll talk about these, all right?"

I don't answer but continue down the short hallway to the bathroom, closing the door softly behind me. The bathroom has become my temporary—very temporary—refuge. I lean against the wall, staring at my reflection in the mirror. I look angry. I feel angry. But what can I do? I just can't make myself walk out. What I want to do and what I'm obligated to do are two different things.

I step to the sink and turn on the water, cupping

my hands underneath the faucet as cold water runs through my fingers. I splash some water on my face, trying to calm my annoyance at the turn my life has taken. When did things spin so completely out of control? I lift my head, looking again at my reflection in the mirror. Time to ask myself a question. Would I have felt this way about Karen and the upcoming marriage if it wasn't for Ashley? If I hadn't read that snippet of her hot, sexy manuscript on her laptop? If she hadn't agreed to my suggestion that she explore the world of bondage with me as her mentor, ostensibly to bring her prose to life?

I don't blame Ashley. No. I blame myself. And why didn't I put my foot down and just refuse to marry Karen when it was first brought up? Since when did I go around trying to please everybody, trying to keep everyone happy?

A headache blossoms behind my eyes. I open the medicine cabinet, thinking to take an aspirin. Amidst the makeup, the Band-Aids, and perfume bottles and lipsticks, I see a bottle of aspirin. I reach for it, then look up at the top shelf. Half-hidden behind some cold medicine I see a orange-brown prescription bottle. Frowning, I move aside the cold medicine and reach for the bottle. I turn it only to find that parts of the label have been smudged, as if it had been held under water and the ink rubbed off.

I read the prescription label and can only make out *Amb*...I look at the name on the prescription, what little I can see of it, and stare. All I can make out of the first and last name is *Car— Que—*.

I frown, not quite sure what I'm looking at, and then it clicks. The Ambien bottle doesn't belong to Karen; it belongs to her mother, Carol. The label was damaged, probably deliberately. The doctor told me that the paramedics found an empty prescription bottle next to Karen on the bed. From there it isn't difficult to come to the conclusion that Karen didn't down the entire bottle. Does she have more of these? Why?

Fury engulfs me as the truth hits me. She faked it. There's nothing in this bottle. There might have been a pill or two or none at all in the bottle the paramedics found, but it was hard to know for sure. It looks to me as if Karen had stolen her mother's empty prescription bottle, perhaps more than one. Then again, for all I know, Karen downed a recently filled prescription, again stolen from her mother. I grasp the prescription bottle in my hand, resisting the urge to crush it in my anger. Only one way to find out.

I open the bathroom door and walk down the hallway and into the dining room. Karen hasn't touched her soup, embroiled in tapping figures out on her calculator. She doesn't even look up. I slam the prescription bottle down onto the table right next to her calculator. She freezes, then slowly looks up at me.

"Tell me the truth, and I mean the fucking truth." I point at the bottle. "The Ambien belongs to your mother. Are you stealing her medication?"

She sputters, "I don't have to steal anything, Daniel, and I certainly don't like your tone."

"Answer me, Karen," I say, striving for calm. "How much did you take that night?"

She doesn't say anything for several moments, and I know it. My heart pounds in disbelief. "You faked the suicide attempt?" My voice rises. "You *faked* it?"

That's all it takes. I can't believe the change that comes over her. So calm one moment, face flushed with guilt or anger and eyes glaring the next. She stiffens in her chair and then leans back, pointing a finger at me.

"You made a promise to me! You made a promise to my family! Do you think I was going to let you get away with making me—making them—look foolish?"

I stand, stunned.

"You think you're so smart, Daniel. But you know what? I know about your supposedly secret house. I know you bring women there. I know about your perverted..." She pauses with a grimace of distaste. "In fact, I know you took a woman there just couple of days before I ended up in the hospital. I also know it's going to stop. You hear me? It's going to stop. You and that skanky brunette girlfriend of yours... so pathetic."

I take a step back away, not because I'm afraid of her but because I want to slap her. I've never struck a woman in my life, and I don't want to. But I'm shocked. And pissed off. I don't particularly care if she knows about my secret life, but what angers me is the fact that she obviously had me followed. I can't decide whether

I'm more disgusted, annoyed, or... this is the last straw. She faked a suicide attempt to get her own way.

I take another step back before I speak. "You did that to my mother? Your so-called suicide attempt? Don't you realize that my mother really cares for you? And your parents? You did that to the people who love you?" I shake my head. "I can't forgive you for that."

She merely stares back up at me, emotionless. I take a deep breath, realizing I don't want to waste one more bit of emotion on her. I shake my head, my eyes never leaving hers.

"We're done, Karen. For good this time. And I swear, if you pull another stunt like you did last week, not only will your parents find out, but I'll press charges. You hear me?"

She snorts. "You can't press charges on someone who tries to kill themselves."

"Don't push me," I threaten, and I mean every word. "At the very least, I can insist that you get put on a seventy-two-hour psychiatric hold."

"You son of a bitch, you can't do this to me! You can't do this to my family—"

"Watch me," I say. I turn my back on her and leave her apartment, slamming the door shut behind me. I hear something crash against the door—shattering glass, and imagine she's probably thrown the bowl of soup at it. Crazy bitch.

I quickly head downstairs to my car, pulling my phone from my pocket. I press speed dial as I step from the building into the parking garage.

"Hi, Daniel, how are you doing?"

"Mom, I've had it with her. We're done."

"Daniel?"

"She faked her suicide attempt, Mom. She faked it!" My mother says nothing, and I can just imagine the look on her face. "I've always tried to do what you wanted me to do, and until recently, I've been accepting of your wishes. I've compromised on things I never should have compromised on. I wanted to make you happy by marrying Karen, but I can't do it."

Nothing comes over the phone and for a second I wonder if the call dropped. Then I hear her voice, soft with dismay.

"Are you sure, Daniel? She faked her suicide attempt?"

"I'm sure, Mom. I just wanted to let you know in case she tries to call and give you another sob story. I have a feeling she might call you."

"I don't understand..."

"I'm trying to understand it all as well. Are you at home?"

"Yes."

"I'm on my way. We'll talk."

I disconnect the call and continue toward my car. One thing is certain. I'm not marrying Karen. I don't care what kind of histrionics she produces. I've found someone that I want to be with, and I just hope it isn't too late to fix the mess I've made out of things.

24

ASHLEY

I glance up at the clock on the wall. Four o'clock on a Saturday afternoon. Just like old times, sitting in my apartment in frumpy sweats and a T-shirt, working on my laptop. Well, trying to anyway.

It's been a week since Daniel rushed out of my apartment to go rescue Karen. I shouldn't feel so resentful, but I can't help it. What did she have that I didn't? Money? Good looks? A fancy lineage? Big deal. It's funny though; I'm angrier at Karen, a woman I've never met, let alone seen, than I am with Daniel.

He can't help it if his fiancée, ex-fiancée, was weak-minded, or so desperate to hang onto him that she resorted to a suicide attempt to keep him by her side. Sad, really. I know Daniel was trying to do the right thing even though I didn't want to feel that way. His traditional values and loyalty seem at odds with his underground life. The Master, the Dom, and his playroom, as opposed to the professional and solid business owner, fiancée, and future husband.

I stare at my computer screen, dissatisfied and frustrated. I quit trying to revise my first manuscript, the one based on Daniel and me as its main characters. Looking back, I realize now how obvious I was in describing not only appearance, but character and personality. Now I'm working on a second novel; nothing that hints at my life or his. Nothing about the characters based on me, Daniel, or anyone else I knew. The problem is that they seem flat and two-dimensional. I know I can write. I just need some inspiration. Unfortunately, my inspiration flew out the window at about the same pace that Daniel left my apartment last week.

It's a book about a couple venturing into the world of bondage, so it's the same niche, and this time I can write from actual experience. The location of my new story is far from my own, set in a nondescript, one-bedroom community in suburban Los Angeles. The female character of my new book doesn't work in a publishing house, but rather as a realtor in swanky Beverly Hills. My main male character is nothing like Daniel, but one that I've developed as a rather introverted mechanic. You don't have to be rich to delve into bondage, and I want to stay away from any similarities in my character or the slowly developing plot line from my first book.

DURING THE PAST WEEK, I've had to force myself to go to work and act as if nothing is wrong. Act like the past few months of my life haven't been an out-of-control roller coaster ride—first admiring and crushing on Daniel from afar, then indulging in a torrid underground affair with him. Tory told me that word floating around the pub house was that Daniel was called away for some kind of family emergency. I pretended disinterest, other than the initial *oh I'm sorry to hear about that* offer of sympathy. Inside, my curiosity was killing me. What happened with Karen?

Things returned to normal, at least at work. After the third day, I found myself glancing down the hallway toward Daniel's office less frequently. By the fifth night, I could lay in bed and try to go to sleep without imagining a bondage scene with Daniel standing behind me, his cock pressed up against my ass, my pussy wet with desire and anticipation.

By yesterday, I was beginning to grow disgruntled with myself. Let him go! He doesn't want you! So, here I am, forcing myself to concentrate on new beginnings; a new story, a new attitude, and... well, if not exactly a new life, then a new outlook.

I admit that I miss Daniel, but focusing on creating a new manuscript is keeping me occupied and in a way, does make me feel better. This time, when describing bondage scenes, I know exactly what I'm talking about. I'm writing what I know, one of the foundations of authorship.

I do wish that someday, I'll be able to finish my first

book, but I'm not so sure how to do it without thinking of Daniel. That character *is* Daniel. Putting it away for a time seems like a good idea, even though I hate to do it. At the same time, I know that if I don't, I'll end up wallowing, and I don't want to do that either.

Daniel taught me plenty, and I appreciate that. I told myself that when he returns to work, more than likely a married man, I'll treat him with the same courtesy and respect with which I've always treated him. I won't hold a grudge, fuss or internally whine. After all, we had an agreement. It isn't his fault that I ended up falling for him, wishing...

A knock on my door startles me. I jolt upright in my chair, staring at the door. I hear nothing from the other side. I rise from my chair and walk toward the door, thinking how wonderful it would be if this was a moment of *déjà vu* and I would open it to find Daniel standing on the other side. I'm not really surprised when I open the door and find a UPS delivery man wearing his brown uniform, a package in one hand, his digital boxlike gadget in the other.

He shoves the contraption toward me. "Sign here, please."

I almost laugh at my foolish wishful thinking as I grab the stylus hanging from the device, scribble my name on the screen, then hand it back to him while he hands me a large, white plastic envelope. He turns and walks down the hallway as I step back into my apartment. I close and lock the door before turning the envelope in my hand. It has the typical mailing stickers on it, but in the shadowed light of my small foyer, I can't see the return address.

I take it into the living room and sit down on the couch, pulling the plastic mailer open. I peek inside and see a stack of paper about an inch thick. A manuscript? I reach inside and pull it out, realizing that it's a printed copy of *my* manuscript. I frown, thumbing through it. I know that Daniel had to be the sender, and a surge of emotion sweeps upward. Unexpected and powerful. Is this his way of saying goodbye? Sending me my manuscript as if to say he wants nothing more to do with me? Oh, how I wish everything worked out. Maybe—

Wait a minute. As I thumb through the pages, I remember that I ended my draft on Chapter Twenty. As I flip toward the end of the manuscript, I see a Chapter Twenty-One, and another after that. My manuscript ended on the Saturday evening before Christmas. The last chapter heading here is the second week in January. I frown and lean back. Today is January fifteenth. Curious, I begin to read the last two chapters. My eyes widen as I realize that Daniel must have written the additional chapters, adding several scenes to my story that tell how the hero met someone; someone who understood him, didn't expect anything from him, and wanted only to please him, not only in the bedroom, or his playroom basement, but as a partner.

I choke back a lump in my throat when I read the last few pages. The hero broke up with his fiancée after she faked a suicide attempt in a desperate ploy to keep him despite knowing that he was interested in, and falling in love with, someone else. My heartbeat begins to accelerate as I read further. The hero called off his engagement a second time, swearing to the fiancée that he was going to try to win the heroine back.

I turn the page, anxious to see how Daniel ended the story, but to my intense frustration, it's blank.

"What the hell!"

Another knock on the door startles me. Did the delivery man forget something? Placing the manuscript on the coffee table, I stand and hurry to the door. When I open it, my heart leaps into my throat. Daniel. I blink, so surprised I can't say anything for several moments. He stands there, looking at me, not saying a word.

"You wrote those two chapters, didn't you?" I barely get the words out. I want to leap into his arms on the one hand and guard myself and my heart on the other.

"Yes, I did." He nods.

I can't help it. Once again, my heart burgeons with hope. "Is it true? What you wrote?"

He nods again. "Very much so."

I step back, allowing him entry. He brushes past me, and I inhale a whiff of his intoxicating cologne. I shut the door and turn to find him standing close, so close that I feel his heat, intoxicated by his nearness.

"Why isn't there an ending?" I ask. He smiles at me; a tender, smile that literally has my nipples tingling.

"Because the ending will be up to you."

Is this for real? I resist the urge to pinch myself, all the while staring up into his grass-green eyes, gazing somberly, yet with affection down at me. Life is filled with ups and downs, risks and challenges, and I know that the only way to find out for sure is to take that step.

"I've always been a sucker for a happily ever after ending," I say.

"And how would the ending go?"

I step closer, place my hands against his chest, then trail them downward. Brazenly, I sweep one hand down further along his hip, then along the inside of his thigh to cup his manhood. "I'd end it with a bang." I grin.

He laughs and wraps his arms around me, hugging me close. I revel in his embrace. I have no idea where things will go from here, but I'm willing to take a chance.

"I have to admit that I'm relieved, and more than happy to hear that's what you want," he says.

I feel his hand lifting my chin and his lips lower toward mine. We kiss; not a desperate kiss, but a gentle, tender, and heartfelt caress that has my knees going weak. Finally, with my pulse throbbing in my neck and my breath hitching in my throat, he leans back.

"I still want to publish your book, Ashley, but we still have to figure some things out."

"We can talk about all that later," I say. "Right now, I just want my happy-ending."

And a happy-ending I got.

THE END

Turn the page to start reading VIP: Taken By The Billionaire.

VIP: TAKEN BY THE BILLIONAIRE

VIP: TAKEN BY THE BILLIONAIRE – SNEAK PEAK:

Chapter 1 – Daniela

Another day, another dollar.

That's what I tell myself as I clean a glass and place it carefully underneath the bar at Trinity, a local dive in Chicago. I wash another one, doing my best to ignore the creep who continues to edge toward me from his side of the bar.

"Hey, baby, come on," he says, cocking his head, his hands straying closer to me. "When do you finish your shift? We could get a drink."

"I'm good," I respond calmly, but I'm starting to get pissed. He's been at this for the last half hour, and since I'm the only bartender on duty right now, I'm an easy target. At this time of day, there's only a handful of other people scattered around the room. The odd couple having a conversation in hushed tones next to the window, and a woman drinking alone at the other end of the bar.

"What can I do to convince you?" he whines, sounding like a toddler denied his favorite toy.

Okay, now I'm getting seriously pissed.

I slam down the wine glass I'm cleaning on the bar between us. "I'm not interested. Okay, buddy?" I lower my eyebrows, giving him my best glower. "Either cut it out or go to another bar."

Of course, the universe immediately punishes me for standing up for myself.

As soon as the words are out of my mouth, he raises his hands in a defensive gesture and knocks the glass off the edge of the bar. Even as I reach for it, I know that I should just let it smash, clean it up, and use it as an excuse to kick his ass out. But instead, on instinct, I try to catch it. As I lunge forward, it hits one of the shelves beneath the bar, cracks into several pieces, and a large fragment spins off, landing a deep cut between my thumb and forefinger.

"Motherfucker!" I yell, too annoyed with myself to register the pain as blood begins to drip steadily from the gash in my hand. My eyes shoot up, and the guy's face goes white. He quickly looks away, pretending he doesn't see the chaos he created.

"Asshole," I mutter to myself as I grab a towel and head toward the employee bathroom to clean up.

As I run the water, I'm so focused on my hand that I barely notice Tina enter the room. She must have just gotten in to join me for the evening rush. She's been mixing drinks here at Trinity Sports Bar for as long as I've known her and is actually the one who recommended me to the manager.

"Shit, Daniela!" She takes my wrist and pulls it towards her. "What happened?"

"Nothing," I mumble, but she's already leading me through to the staffroom.

"I'm getting you bandaged up," she says firmly and reaches for the first aid kit. I feel my head start to swim as I watch her try to fix me up. The blood doesn't seem to want to stop.

"What's going on in here?" Dennis, the manager, appears at the door. He sounds even more pissed off than usual.

"Uh, there was a guest out there." I nod toward the bar. "He was hassling me, and–"

"He says you went crazy on him." Dennis raises his eyebrows and crosses his arms. "Says you threw a glass at his head."

"Jesus Christ, Dennis. Can't you see how badly hurt she is?" Tina snaps. Dennis shoots her a look, and she quiets down. She needs this job as much as the rest of us, no matter how much of an asshole our boss is.

"Is that true? Did you throw a glass at him? Is that how you got that cut?"

"Bullshit!" An unfamiliar voice enters the equation. "That's so not what happened."

We all turn, and Dennis steps aside to reveal the only other woman in the bar standing behind him. She's taller than she looked sitting down.

"I saw everything," she continues. "That asshole was the one who shoved the glass off the counter. She went to catch it, and that's when she got hurt."

She shoots me a conciliatory look, and I nod back with a grateful smile. With only a few words, my ass is officially saved.

The woman steps into the room. "He's really drunk. I don't even think he should be in here, but yeah...it was totally that guy's fault."

"Thanks for your help." Dennis plasters on his prime customer-pleasing grin. He turns to me with a rare look of apology on his face. "I'll get him chucked out," he mumbles and then gestures to my hand. "You should get that looked at. Take the rest of the day off."

***

After the nurse practitioner at the urgent care center dumped a glob of what looked like superglue in my cut and steri-stripped it together, I'm on my way with a warning to keep the wound dry for a couple of days and watch out for signs of infection. A nice tetanus shot rounds out the visit, and I know I'll feel that muscle for a while.

"Thanks, Mom," I mutter, feeling petulant and childish, but unable to help myself. I love my mom, but she checked out of this world a couple years ago, overtaken by bouts of depression so deep she's been hospitalized several times. I have great sympathy for her illness, but sometimes, I just need my mother to answer the phone. I miss talking to her and asking things as simple as when my last vaccinations were.

Guilt immediately follows these negative thoughts, and I cross the street, heading to the nursing home located down the block. Outside its doors, I take a deep breath and plaster a smile on my face.

"Hi, Judy," I say to the receptionist as I sign in.

The older lady gives me a motherly grin. "Hi, Daniela. You're here awfully early today."

I hold up my bandaged hand, and her smile fades away. "It's no big deal. Just got me out of work earlier than usual."

She gives me the same *watch out for infection* lecture I'd just endured, then buzzes me through the security door. I walk the familiar hallway, then bounce up the stairs until I'm on the third-floor residence hall. Here, the living accommodations are more like apartments and couples can live together in the space with minimal assistance from the staff. When we moved to Chicago a couple years ago, finding this place was like a miracle for both of my parents.

Outside of their room, I take another deep breath and gently push open the door. Mom is lying on her bed, curled up in a tight ball while Dad watches TV from his, the dialysis machine churning its blood cleansing wheels beside him.

"Hey, Dani-bean," Dad calls out when he sees me. I frown at how pale he is. I plaster on the smile again and walk over to his bed. He clicks off the television and pats the mattress for me to take a seat next to him. I do and am soon enfolded next to his warmth – the safest place I've ever known.

"How are you feeling?" I ask him after a few minutes, but already know what his answer will be.

"Fine and dandy," we say together and laugh. It's the same response I get every day.

Diagnosed as a teenager with what was then called juvenile diabetes, his disease has been progressively working on his kidneys until it became clear that a transplant was his only option. I hug him tighter, willing his name to miraculously jump up higher on the donor list before his body is too weak for the operation. Normal wait time is four to six years, and he's already been on the list for nearly three.

I stay until he grows tired, then kiss him on the forehead and say my goodbyes. I step over to Mom's bed and give her a kiss too, wishing there was an operation that could fix the progressive deterioration of her mind and spirit.

Minutes later, I'm sitting in a cab on the way back to my apartment. Well, *our* apartment – it still feels weird to think of it that way. Pete and I have been dating almost two years and have lived together for one. We met at a club where he was DJing. I was tending the bar and we bumped into each other when we both headed outside for a break. The rest is history.

Before we met, I was living in a cramped apartment with three roommates, so moving in with him saved my sanity. I look at my watch and smile. Pete should still be home, and I could use a little sanity saving right now.

Pete is a self-diagnosed sex addict, and he never

stops going at it. If I just hint that I'm in the mood, he'll be rubbing up on me in a nanosecond. Even though he's twenty-four now, he still has the libido of a fifteen-year-old who's just seen his first pair of tits.

I squirm in my seat just thinking about being with him. He's by far the hottest guy I've ever slept with, although that's not saying much. There wasn't exactly a wide choice of sex gods back in my little hometown of Pella, Iowa. So when Pete entered my life, all muscles and cropped hair and cheekbones, I felt as though I'd hit some crazy lottery. Yeah, he's not the smartest, and he flirts too much with other women, but hey, with that body and face, I can't complain.

I'm ready for something wild...maybe anal? Pete always asks, but we've never actually done it because I'm nervous it might hurt. But today, a little pain, followed by a delightful orgasm, might just be what the doctor ordered to make me forget this entire day. I run my fingers through my hair and pull out my phone, inspecting myself using the selfie camera. I look a mess, but a dab of makeup will cover up the worst.

I pay the driver and hop out of the cab, fumbling awkwardly with my opposite hand in my pocket to find my keys. I unlock the door and sashay my way up the stairs, doing my best to feel sexy as I open the door to the apartment. That's when I hear it.

The unmistakable sound of sex coming from our bedroom.

Bedsprings are creaking rhythmically, and Pete's small moans of pleasure echo throughout the house. I close the door quietly, not sure how to react, and make my way across the hall. I press my ear to the bedroom door, and I could swear that...

Before I can finish my thought, the door flies open, and I tumble into the room. I gape at the display before me. Pete is standing in front of me, stark naked, and in our bed is a...*guy*. The covers are pulled haphazardly around him so I can't see if he's naked too, but I'm not stupid enough to place money against that one.

My face feels numb as all the blood drains into my toes. I open my mouth to say something–

"I'm sorry," he blurts out before I can utter a sound. "I thought you were at work."

"S-so?" I manage to say, clutching my hand, which has started to emit a low dull throbbing in rhythm to my pounding heart.

"So..." He gestures to the guy behind him. "I know I should have told you sooner–"

I begin to snap back into reality. "Wait, how long has this been going on?"

"Uh, a couple weeks?" Pete flashes me a smile as if I'm just going to roll over and take this.

"And is he the first...?" I trail off, not sure whether I should specify gender. I'm too shell-shocked to really know what I need to find out.

"Uh, yeah," Pete runs a hand through his hair, and I can see that he's lying.

"Hey, you want to join us or not?" The guy in the bed props up on his elbows and raises his eyebrows at me.

My mouth opens in disbelief, but nothing comes out. Again, I'm speechless.

Pete scratches the stubble on his chin. "Could be fun."

"Fuck you!" I snap, finding my anger at last. "I'm leaving."

"When will you be back?" Pete asks casually as if this is nothing more than a mild disagreement.

"I won't," I snarl. "We're done."

"Dani, wait!" he calls as I storm out of the room. I ignore him and slam the door so hard I hear the bed shake. I'll come back later to pick up my stuff, but right now, I need to get the hell away from here.

I make it down to the street before it hits me. Just like that, I'm single again. And homeless. I don't cry, which surprises me. After my last breakup, I bawled my eyes out for a full week, and we'd only been together six months. I guess somewhere in the back of my mind, I always suspected that Pete wasn't entirely faithful, but his bisexuality, well, that was a surprise.

It's a hot and humid Chicago day, and the sweat is pouring off me as I walk fast, barely noticing my surroundings. I'm trying to put as much space as I possibly can between my cheating ex-boyfriend and me.

I look up and realize that I'm outside of work. The faded Trinity Bar sign sits a few feet over my head, and I sigh when I think about what this says about me. My safe place is my job? That's shitty. Since I'm here, I might as well find out if I can make up the hours I missed earlier. My hand feels better, and I could sure use the extra tips.

Inside, it's even more humid than on the streets. The crowds are gathering for the Friday night drinking marathon. I squeeze through the reams of people, exchanging a few loaded looks with a couple of cute guys who give me the up and down. I can't imagine I'm looking my best, but I appreciate the attention.

Dennis has left, replaced by Sheila, the night manager. Everyone prefers her to the asshole because she's a lot easier to get along with.

"Hey, Sheila." I stick my head into her office, and she jolts slightly at my appearance.

"Surprised to see you here," she says and leans back in her seat. "Dennis told me you had a pretty nasty accident earlier today. He sent you to the ER, right?"

"Yeah." I fight the urge to roll my eyes at the mere mention of Dennis's name. "But I'm all put together again, and I've got the evening off, so I thought–?"

"If you think I'm going to let you out there on a Friday night with your hand sliced and diced, you've got another thing coming." Sheila gets to her feet and steps toward me. "Come on. Go home, get some rest. Get that cute and sexy boyfriend of yours to look after you."

I try to hide the look of disappointment on my face. "Sure," I mumble, not ready to share the news of our break-up with anyone. I sidle back into the bar, scanning the place. Time to change my luck. I've had a creep coming on to me, an accident that sent me to the emergency room, and a break-up with my boyfriend of two years, all in one day. As my old daddy always says – *when life hands you lemons, make whiskey sour*.

I push my way through to the bar and lean on the counter, catching Tina's eye. She quickly heads my way and deftly pours a shot into a small glass, shoving it toward me.

"This will help. How's your hand?" She frowns sympathetically.

"They just dumped some of that glue stuff in it. It's nothing, really." I offer her my best fake smile and reach for the drink with my bad hand – wincing. I withdraw it and use the other to toss back the shot.

"Be careful. You'll tear it open. I've got to serve that group over there," Tina nods to a table at the other side of the bar, "but I'll catch you soon, yeah?"

"Sure thing."

I watch her leave and fight the urge to reach over the bar and pour myself another shot. One thing is certain, after this long fucked-upped day, all I want to do is get wasted.

"Are you okay?"

I jump as a soft hand lands on my shoulder. I turn and see the woman who defended me earlier. I give her a smile. "Yeah, thanks. I really appreciate you stepping up for me."

She holds out a hand. "I'm Aria," she says as she takes a seat beside me.

I'm grateful that my wound is on my left hand as we shake. "Daniela."

"Are you sure you're okay," she asks, eyeing me closely. "You seem...upset."

I'm not sure why, but I feel tears prick the back of my eyes. I blink hard, willing them away.

Aria squeezes my fingers. "Oh, honey, want to talk about it?"

I look into her eyes and realize I do. Maybe talking to a stranger will be easier than with a friend.

As I spill my story, Aria orders us both a straight whiskey.

"I didn't even know he was bi," I complain and take a sip.

She winks at me. "Nothing wrong with that," she says with a laugh.

I laugh too and the stress of the day seems to float away. Maybe it's the effects of the whiskey, but I think it's more that I'm able to get all this burden off my chest.

"Thanks for listening to all that," I tell her and raise my glass in a silent toast.

She clinks her glass to mine. "Anytime. And speaking of anytime, how about this weekend?"

I look at her curiously. "What do you mean?"

She leans closer. "My aunt has this amazing house down in Fort Lauderdale, Florida. I'm heading down there this weekend for a party but I hate traveling alone. You should come with me. Plenty of hot and sexy guys. Nothing like getting your mind off a guy than a quick fling with another guy."

I smile. "That sounds incredible, but right now, I can't even afford a McDonalds happy meal, much less a plane ticket."

"Oh, honey." Aria laughs. "You'll be so glad you met me. I've got like two million flying miles saved up. We'll get you a ticket."

I look up from the amber liquid I'd been staring at and meet Aria's eyes. "Seriously?"

Aria nods. "Seriously."

It's tempting. Florida does sound better than Chicago any day of the week.

"Come on," Aria says as I hesitate. "The ocean. Hot guys. Free getaway with a new friend. How can you say no to all that?"

How indeed?

Get your free ebook copy of VIP: Taken By the Billionaire!

To download, go to:

www.tashafawkes.com/get-your-free-book/

ABOUT TASHA FAWKES

I'm originally from a small southern town where everyone knew everyone and their business. I was so happy to leave and move to California for college where I was originally going to be a veterinarian.

Well, I met a guy – yeah, it's that kind of story – and dropped out of school to have my oldest daughter. We soon divorced, and as a kind of therapy, I started to write books. I loved the fantasy world of ction and never did go back to college, and have been writing ever since.

I write about sexy guys and girls. Anything but missionary – unless the heroine is tied up tight. My southern upbringing sure brings the kinkiness out of me. Don't be shy to stay in touch. I'd love to hear your kinky stories. Maybe we can turn them into a book. :)

XXX, Tasha

Please visit me at and get a free ebook!
http://tashafawkes.com/

ABOUT M. S. PARKER

M. S. Parker is a USA Today Bestselling author and the author of the Erotic Romance series, Club Privè and Chasing Perfection.

Living in Las Vegas, she enjoys sitting by the pool with her laptop writing on her next spicy romance.

Growing up all she wanted to be was a dancer, actor or author. So far only the latter has come true but M. S. Parker hasn't retired her dancing shoes just yet. She is still waiting for the call for her to appear on Dancing With The Stars.

When M. S. isn't writing, she can usually be found reading– oops, scratch that! She is always writing.

For more information:
www.msparker.com
msparkerbooks@gmail.com

Made in the USA
Monee, IL
26 May 2021